FROM LOST TO FOUND

By
Brenda Seymour

Published by Island Blue Printorium Bookworks
911 Fort Street
Victoria, British Columbia, Canada V8V 3K3

This book is dedicated to those I love the most: my husband, Lorne; our fur babies, Scruffy & Trixie, best dogs ever; and our prickly baby, Tumbleweed, our hedgehog.

To Ed and Lisa, my brother and sister, finding you both has filled that empty spot in my heart and soul, and I love you both dearly. I wish we had all been able to grow up together.

But without my BC Mommy, Cheryle, none of this would be possible.

And to all my friends who have supported me throughout this endeavour, you know who you are, and you know how much you all mean to me. Without all of you behind me I would not have been able to travel through this journey.

Although presented as fiction, this work is based on reality, the life of the author. Names and some of the events have been changed, but all the story is true. Writing this has been like therapy, and has enabled me to put the past where it belongs, in the past. I hope you will enjoy this window into my life, and those that know me personally may come away with a greater understanding of the person I am.

~Brenda Seymour
trixie11@telus.net

"When in doubt, tell the truth"
~Mark Twain

"I seldom end up where I wanted to go, but almost always end up where I need to be."
~Douglas Adams

"Life isn't about waiting for the storm to pass. It's learning to dance in the rain."
~Vivian Greene

Chapter 1

The envelope is in the mail today. I open the box and pull out the envelopes, quickly flipping through all the bills and junk mail, and suddenly stop. Here it is. Finally. Since putting in the paperwork almost six months ago and, honestly, waiting for over thirty years, I will finally know who I am today. It is 11:45 a.m. My husband, Tom, will not be home for at least another four hours. My hands are shaking. My palms are sweating. My breath catches in my throat while my heart feels like it is going to burst out of my chest. I set the envelope by the phone, and decide to wait for Tom to call during his lunch break. When the phone rings forty-five minutes later I am still standing there, staring at the envelope. The time has come.

Tom thinks I should wait until he is home to open it. He thinks I will have some kind of breakdown, and with him at work, there is nothing he can do to help me. I tell him I will be fine, but he is so adamant that I decide to wait. He says he will be home as soon as he can.

I know why he doesn't get it. He is not adopted. I guess unless you are adopted you will not understand. Even then, there are as many stories as there are adoptees and birth parents.

I make a cup of tea and sit by the window, watching the snow fall and thinking about my life.

I have always known that I am adopted. I guess my adoptive parents told me right from the time I could talk, even though at that time I was too young to understand what being adopted meant. Most of my life I felt different. There was something missing inside me. There was an empty space in my heart and soul, yearning to be filled. I knew there was something I needed to do. That something was searching for my birth family, and what is in that envelope will start that search. You see, that envelope contains my "real" name. The first clue to who I am.

When Tom comes home he finds me sitting in that same spot, where I have been thinking about this search, and my mind has run wild. I have gone from envisioning a wonderful reunion with my birth mother, to the complete opposite end of the scale, a horror filled search, where no one wants a reunion. At least no one but me.

He grabs a drink and comes to sit on the window seat with me. His deep brown eyes are searching my face, trying to find clues about my mood. The snow has been falling lightly all afternoon, and the flakes have melted into his hair. I run my fingers through his hair, and he shakes his head. We both laugh. I don't know how many times in the years that I have known him we've laughed over that because I told him once he was like a wet dog that has to shake, no matter where he is, nor the company he is in.

We are done laughing now, and just staring at the elephant in the room. The envelope. If I don't open it, it will always be the elephant. So, I open it, and pull out the contents. The first page is a summary of my adoption order. The second page is the adoption order.

There it is. There's my name. My birth name. My first name has always been Emma. That never changed when the people that fostered me legally adopted me. Now, in black and white, I have a middle name and surname, different from the ones I have now, proof that I was once a "different" person in the eyes of the law. Only for a couple of years, but I was someone else. My name was Emma Jo Quinn. Do I feel like an Emma Jo Quinn?

I did not think that I would feel any different, but I do. I know who I was now. In addition, if I type Quinn into an internet search engine I'm sure I will find other Quinn's. People with the surname Quinn, people who could be my family.

Nevertheless, searching brings up many fears. What if I find my birth mother? What if she doesn't want to meet me? Do I have brothers and sisters? The list goes on and on. I am excited to start looking, but where? Moreover, how?

I sit there, repeating my name over and over, scared to open this can of worms. Part of me wants to search, to find my birth mom, but part of me is scared. Terrified really. If I find her, how will my life change? Will anything ever be the same?

Tom has made his opinion clear. I should be content with knowing my name. My fear, that scared little girl inside me, agrees with him. Once I post this information on the search sites online there is no turning back. It's out there. Somewhere in cyberspace. Out there for everyone to see and maybe recognize. Is my mother looking for me? Does she spend my birthday the same way I do?

Every year I put on the fake smile, look grateful, and excited, surprised, while others wish me Happy Birthday, and give me the gifts they think I want. Meanwhile, in my head, I am somewhere else. I spend the day wondering if she thinks of me at all. Does she ever wonder where I am? Who I am? What I have become?

I have tried over the years, and the multitudes of discussions to understand Tom's position. But I can't. Just like he cannot understand mine. But how dare he? He has no right to tell me I should not look for my birth mother. Does he know what it is like to be adopted? No. Does he wonder who he looks like every time he looks in the mirror? No. Nevertheless, I do, and now I have a name. My name. The one and only thing she gave me.

I can hear him in the kitchen, closing cupboard doors just a little harder than he should, making his anger heard throughout the house. He walks into the office and sits at his desk. I follow him into the office, knowing we need to talk, but not knowing exactly how to start the conversation. I sit down at my desk, and looking over at him, I know he can see all the pain and confusion in my eyes. He glares over at me.

"Emma? Can we talk about this?" he says.

"Why, Tom?" I reply. "We've been talking for hours, years really, and you still can't understand my feelings. What can I say at this point to change your mind that I haven't already said? I just don't think there is anything I can do that is going to make both of us happy. Either you get your way, and I spend more years wondering, not being able to talk to you about it, or I search, still not able to talk to you about it. You, of all people, are supposed to be the one person I can trust to have my back through everything. But I'm on my own here, alone."

He sighs, turns on his computer, and dives into whatever it is that he does there for hours at a time.

With tears in my eyes, I turn off my computer. I walk out of the office, glancing back at my husband, wishing more than anything else that he could see the need in me, and could support me. I feel like I just lost my best friend, my support system.

This search will go on, with or without his support.

Chapter 2

Today is Saturday, and Tom is home this weekend. I get up before him in the morning and sit at the kitchen table drinking coffee and thinking about last night. Tom went to bed early, and when I went to bed a couple of hours later I had the feeling that he was laying there awake, but didn't want me to know. So I didn't let on, I just rolled over and tried to shut my mind off so I could sleep. Today is going to be a busy day. We are hosting a birthday party for our nephew who is turning five. The birthday party is at our house because Tom's sister and her husband just do not have the room at their house for a big party, especially one with lots of kids running around.

Tom comes into the kitchen after I have been sitting there for what seems like hours. No good morning. No good morning kiss. He goes straight for the coffee, and the newspaper that I had brought in and planned to read, but had left sitting on the kitchen counter. He sits at the table hidden behind the newspaper, and I have never felt more alone.

Before the chaos of the day starts, I need to talk to Tom. We need to be able to go through the day without this situation hanging over us, and affecting everyone else's mood. So, I take a deep breath, and say, "Good morning."

He grumbles something incoherent from behind his newspaper.

I try again. "Tom, we need to talk about last night."

"You're right, Emma. We do, and we will." Tom says. "But please, let's get this day over with before we have that talk. Just know that I love you, and I know that last night I probably came across like a caveman, but I have to tell you, it's because I am your husband, and I don't want to see you hurt."

By the time he has finished I am in tears, the tension from last night flowing out of me with each tear. It was a relief to hear him say that. "Okay, that's fair, and you know that you are my world, and I love you with all that I am."

With that being said, Tom put the newspaper down and we had our usual Saturday morning at the kitchen table. We talked about our week, and what was to come next week. Then we settled the agenda for the day as much as we were able to, knowing that if something can go wrong, it will go wrong. At least that's the way our lives seemed to be. Nothing life altering has ever happened, but, to us they always seem like larger than life problems at the time. My feeling at the time was that we had made it through everything that came before, and we would make it through this weekend without any permanent scars.

The party was a hit that day, and every one of the kids went home filthy dirty, with ice cream and cake all over them. To me that meant it was a success, more than my sister-in-law and her husband thanking us and telling us how great the day was. Happy children were a sign of success to me, and there sure were some happy, dirty children leaving our house.

When all the guests had left and we were alone we both fell onto the couch, exhausted. Mostly from the day's events, but some of the exhaustion was due to the sleepless night before. We talked about the party a bit and wondered if we would throw parties like that when we had kids. If we had kids. We had been trying for a while now to get pregnant, and we were not having any luck.

Saturday nights were usually quiet nights for us. We would cuddle on the couch, watching movies, or watching sports, and just have a night of eating munchies, talking, and just being together. Sundays were usually more of the same, although Tom was a big football fan, and I didn't understand the game, so we may not have spent the time together, but we were still home together. This Sunday was a little different. We had to finish all the cleanup from the party the day before and Tom was leaving that Tuesday for a business trip, so we had to make sure he was ready to go. Laundry had to be done along with all the other things that had to be done before he left town. Being a homemaker meant that I would be alone for four days, which, even though it may sound lonely, it was nice for me. No getting up before the crack of dawn to get my husband off to work, and no more big meals to make. Just four days of me doing the things I love to do, on my schedule. Of course, I still had to walk the dogs, but that was something I had always enjoyed doing. The fresh air, and the time alone to think, it was nice.

Late Sunday afternoon, we had finished all the things we needed to do, so I made myself a cup of tea and went back to my favourite spot in the house, the seat by the window. It was snowing again, and staring out at the falling snow was almost mesmerizing. Tom came in a few minutes later with two beers in his hands, and sat down with me on the window seat, offering me one of the beers. I took a long drink. It tasted quite good after the last few days. We sat there in silence for a few minutes, drinking our beers, each thinking our own thoughts.

"Tom," I said after a few minutes, "why are you so against me doing a search for my birth family? I want to understand your feelings about this, and see if there is a middle ground for us."

He thought about it for a minute, and cleared his throat before he began to speak. "Emma, if I could guarantee you a happy ending to this, I would say go ahead, and I would be right there searching with you. Be that as it may, I know how you will invest yourself, physically and emotionally, in this search, and what scares me is the ending. When you reach the end of your search you may not get your happy ending. It scares me because I don't know how much more hurt you can take about being adopted. You don't deserve to be hurt anymore, and I have no way to control that, to protect you from it."

I welled up with tears, just hearing the love and concern in his voice. "Oh sweetheart, I'm so sorry. I never wanted to make you feel this way about my adoption. Nevertheless, that's my life. My story. Maybe my birth family will be, or is, completely different from the family I grew up in. It could turn out wonderful for me, for us, and for my family as well. Couldn't it?"

"Of course it could babe, but I'm sure that not all of the stories end like the ones they show on TV," Tom responded. "I just don't want you to think it is going to be all rainbows and unicorns."

I took a deep breath, and bit my bottom lip. "Tom, I don't know what I expect, and I do appreciate your opinion. You know that you are my best friend, and my world, and I would never do anything to jeopardize that. But there's still that part of me that wonders all the time. Who do I look like? Where are my parents now? Do I have siblings? So many questions that maybe I can finally have answered. Every day for as long as I can remember I have looked in the mirror and wondered who I really am. I know who I was raised to be, and that upbringing has brought me to here and now. With you. Where I want to be, and I can't imagine being anywhere else. This is where I belong. I have no doubt of that, and nothing that I find out will ever shake that confidence. I think it will only make us better together, because I won't be preoccupied with the things that every other person in my life takes for granted. You know exactly who you look like, where you came from. Everything I want to know you have known all your life. Can you imagine not knowing any of it? Right now, right here, you know none of what you know now about your family, your history. Can you even wrap your mind around any of that?"

"No, Emma, I can't. Now that you say it that way, it makes a little more sense to me. I can understand now why it's a need in you that you have to satisfy."

I wrapped my arms around his neck, and started to laugh and cry at the same time. Finally! Someone in my life finally gets it, finally has a small inkling of how I have felt all my life, and wants to understand it. In that moment, I was ecstatic.

That changed quickly. Tom continued to say that he still was not sure that searching was the best option.

So my thinking that someone finally got it was wrong. Maybe not completely wrong, but wrong enough that he still doesn't get it. I honestly do not think he ever will. How could he? After all, he's not adopted.

We talked some more about it, and finally came to a decision. The decision was that we would not decide tonight. We would take the week to think about it. With Tom being away, and my being here alone, we would both have lots of time to think about it, and come up with all the reasons for and against searching. I agreed to sit down and sketch out a very rough draft of my life with my adopted family. Not day-by-day, or even year by year, but event by event. The good, the bad, and the ugly. On paper. No longer trapped in my memories. I wasn't sure that I would be able to do it, but I promised to do my best. It was a daunting task. I hated to admit it, but I was scared, and I told Tom so. I was scared of all the crappy memories this was going to bring up, and my reaction to them. Was I going to fall apart? On the other hand, would I have a clinical approach to it, try to detach myself from it, and get through it that way? There could be some sleepless nights in my very near future, and I would not have Tom beside me to ease the pain. However, I promised him I would do this. So do this I must.

Brenda Seymour

If I ever wanted to be able to search, and still keep my marriage, I had to do this.

Chapter 3

Tuesday morning Tom left on his business trip, and I was ready to start. On Monday, I had gone to the store, and I had bought two notebooks. One for Tom and one for myself.

After I cleaned the house, walked the dogs, and tried to find more things to do that would keep me from having to go to the table and face that notebook, I was finally out of excuses. At least good ones.

So I made a pot of tea, and sat down, ready to start writing. But where to begin? Everything was so muddled up and confused in my mind. A memory from early childhood would bring up a memory from college, somewhere in between the two, or beyond college. Right now, not one of these is a good memory, and that scares me. Regardless, I force myself to go on. I open the book. One page has "PROS" at the top, and the other has "CONS" at the top. Tom will find a notebook in his suitcase when he unpacks. On the first page, I had written "PROS" at the top. On the very last page I had written "CONS" at the top. On a note stuck to the cover of the notebook, I had written "Here is a book for you to write your reasons in. The good, the bad, and yes, the ugly too. Leave nothing out; I need to know all of your thoughts, even if you think they are silly. Love Always, Emma" with a P.S. "Come home safely to us. We will all miss you. Until Friday."

If only I had known how my life would change that week. As we said, the good, the bad, and everything in between. Yes, the ugly too.

Chapter 4

On Wednesday morning, I woke up in a very thoughtful mood. I had my shower and coffee, and tried to come up with a plan of action for the day. I started to think about this search, and the journey it could take me on. I looked at the book on the kitchen table, still empty, no pros or cons of this search. I think I had already decided that I was going to do this search, whether the outcome was good or bad. I knew Tom. I knew he would come around and support me, no matter whether I was happy or devastated by the outcome.

I opened the book I had for my reasoning, and realized that I could have used maybe one sheet of writing paper for one of the lists, the cons, as far as I was concerned. I know there are good memories from my childhood, just not many, and certainly not more than the bad. I laughed to myself and thought that a psychiatrist could make a lot of money with me as a patient.

I started to write. PRO: To settle the what if's in my mind. Shouldn't that cover all of it? In my mind it did. Good, bad, or ugly, the finale of the search could answer all my questions.

Tom had called me the night before to say he had reached the conference safe, that the hotel room was great, but lonely without me, and that he had found the notebook. He said he would work on it as much as he could, but it was going to be a busy week for him. If only I had known then what he was saying.

My mom was a librarian. It was a small community library, and it was only open ten or twelve hours a week. Books were always a big part of my life, and they were an escape for me. To this day I am still an avid reader. Reading is a relaxation for me. If I don't have a book I feel like something is missing. Sometimes it drives Tom crazy because I don't go anywhere without a book. I might not get a chance to read where ever I'm going, but at least I have it with me should the opportunity arise.

I glanced at the book I was reading at the time, but forced myself to leave it be, and work on the task at hand. It was slow going, but once I got started the memories flooded my mind, and before I realized how long I had been sitting there, it was dark outside, and the day was almost over. I got up from my chair and looked at my puppies. They had been so patient with me all day long. They deserved a nice long walk, and some attention. So off we went, walking and playing in the snow, clearing my mind, and just being in the moment.

After I had some dinner I felt the book calling out to me, so I poured myself a glass of wine and went back to it. In the back of my mind I wondered why Tom hadn't called me today, but I decided he must be having fun, which he deserved to do. After that I never gave it another thought. Until the next evening that is.

Chapter 5

I was tired Thursday morning when I got out of bed because I had spent most of the night writing. It was cathartic, and when I did finally go to bed I was asleep in minutes because my mind was more settled than I ever remember it being. I walked the dogs, and had my breakfast. I was hoping that today would be as productive as yesterday had been.

I decided this was the day to start searching on the internet for ways to start this search. I opened Bing and typed in "adoption search Ontario". I stared at the screen dumbfounded. Over eight million pages. Where do I start? I looked at the first ten options, and decided that I would look at those pages one by one to see if they were any help.

The second link I clicked on looked interesting from the few first lines that I could see on Bing. When the page loaded my jaw dropped to the floor. More links to more pages? I started to feel overwhelmed and had to come up with a plan of action. But how? And where to start? I decided it was time for more coffee; I was going to need it today. My mind was going a hundred miles a minute with thoughts, new information, and this niggling worry kept creeping in. I hadn't heard from Tom last night, and that definitely was not normal. We may spend time apart, but we always kept in contact. I looked at the clock, it was almost 11 am. I doubted very much that he would be in his room, and we didn't yet have cell phones. I called his room anyway, and was not surprised to get the voice mail. I left him a short message to say we missed him, and couldn't wait for him to be home Friday. With that done I put the thought out of my mind. For now.

I walked around and tidied things, thinking about those websites the whole time. After an hour or so of doing mindless tasks a plan had begun to take shape in my mind. The page that I clicked on to find more links was calling to me for some reason. I went back to it, and started a spreadsheet. I would record every webpage, along with any usernames and passwords that I had to register, along with what information I was able to garner from each site. Some sites were registries, so I had to decide if I was going to do that as well today. I decided I would. So each page took me anywhere from five minutes to thirty, depending on the reading to be done, and the information to be posted. Time flew by once again that day, and when the phone rang it was closing in on 5 pm. I got that excited feeling before I looked at the call display, figuring that it was Tom. I missed him terribly, and just hearing his voice always made my day when he was away on business. The name on the call display was a letdown. It wasn't Tom. It was a number I knew all too well, and I had no desire to answer the call. But I had to, it was my Mom. I took a deep breath and hit the talk button.

"Hi Mom."

"Emma, I need to have a word with you, and you need to listen to me before you speak," she said in a stern tone of voice.

I knew that tone all too well. It was never good. So I remained silent, waiting for the barrage. It came fast and furious.

"When you sent a letter, or whatever it's called on the computer, to your sister-in-law she informed me that you sent away for a document regarding your adoption. I am very angry about that. I have told you over and over that you have no right to look for that woman. She gave you up. She didn't want you, so why are you so insistent on ruining her life by barging into it?"

I was starting to shake, and tears were welling up in my eyes.

She wasn't done.

"You are causing nothing but trouble once again, and I suppose I should not be surprised. You have spent your life doing just the opposite of what you know is right. All your life you have fought against me, doing anything you possibly could to tarnish the family name. Do you hear me? You left your first husband, and embarrassed me because now I have a daughter that is divorced. I was hoping that it would end there. But no. You went on to find some guy on the internet, and marry him. No one knows him, or anything about him. But you expect us all just to accept it and move on, going along with you over the cliff. Well we aren't going to this time. We have had enough. From this point on you are on your own. Make all the mistakes you want, which we both know will be many, but don't you dare bring anymore shame and embarrassment to this family. You are so selfish, you don't think of how your decisions are going to reflect on me. I thought I raised you better, but something went wrong. Did you ever think that maybe SHE somehow knew that you would turn out this way and didn't want you because of that? Possibly your father did as well, since he ran out on her while she was pregnant."

By this time I was in shock, and sobbing. I was trying so hard to not let her hear me sniffling. I'm sure she did though. How could she not know that she would be tearing me up? Of course I remembered my first husband. He was an alcoholic, and the beginning of the end of our marriage started the day he laid a hand on me in anger. From that day on I knew I would leave him. We tried counseling, but all he did was blame me for everything. He took no responsibility for his actions. I had no choice. It was either leave or stay and continue to be abused by him, physically and emotionally. Where was the ending if I stayed? Maybe with my death, but I knew I had more to do in my lifetime, and refused to let that happen. I thought Mom was over that. Apparently not. As I processed this my mind froze. Did she just say that my father ran out on my mother when she was pregnant? How did she know that? Anytime I had asked her while I was growing up if she knew anything about my birth parents she said no, nothing other than the fact that my parents weren't married. Obviously that wasn't true. I wanted to scream by that point. I wanted to be able to grab her and make her hear me. I wanted answers, but, I knew I would never get them. I guess the first embarrassment I caused her was not being her blood relative.

While I was processing this information she continued to yell. I stopped listening, and wanted so badly to hang up on her, but I just couldn't do it. She was still my Mom after all. Good or bad, I couldn't change that. I knew that she would never "get it", and I had to accept that and move on. I certainly knew I couldn't tell anyone in my family anything I did from here on in because they felt the need to report it to Mom. I had specifically asked my sister-in-law NOT to say anything to Mom, but I should have known better. She had always felt the need to compete with me when it came to my Mom. I don't know why, but she did, and she had just betrayed my trust for the last time. I had suspected over the years that she was the one filling my Mom's head with information about me and my life. Things that she had no right repeating and things that I still, to this day, do not know how she found out. I certainly hadn't told her many of them, and yet, she knew.

I finally realized there was silence on the other end of the line. "H-h-h-ello? Mom?" No response. She had hung up on me, and I had stood there dazed not realizing it. I stared at the phone, and felt the tears coming again. I had to cry this out so I curled up on my bed, with the dogs, and had a long cry. My dogs always had a way of taking away the hurt. They just loved me unconditionally, the kind of love I wished I could get from my Mom. The tears stopped relatively quickly, considering the hurt and insults that had just been hurled at me. When they stopped the anger started. I felt so alone, and my emotions were all over the place. I needed to talk to my husband, to tell him what had just happened, and to talk it through. He could always calm me down, and helped me see her for what she was. But a thought popped into my head just as I started to dial his hotel number. He might not see it my way this time. His reaction to my searching in the first place had not been favourable, and he might actually agree with my Mom this time. I knew that he would never treat me the way she had, but, it could turn into a conversation I didn't really want to have. I hung up the phone and sat in the window seat with the dogs. I asked them what I should do. Should I call Daddy? At the mention of his name their tails started to wag furiously, and they ran to the door. I had done it now. They thought he was out there, and I had to distract them from that thought. So I walked into the kitchen and opened "their" cupboard. For some reason I could open any cupboard door in the house other than theirs and they wouldn't have any reaction of any kind. But that cupboard door they knew. Was it a smell? Or was it a sound? I would never know, but they sure did come running when that cupboard was opened. I gave them some bones to chew on, and soon enough they forgot all about what I had said.

I decided I would like a glass of wine, so I sat on the couch, and lit a candle. Sitting there in the peace, with the candlelight, and my puppies happily chewing away on the bones, I suddenly felt very lonely, and alone. I picked up the phone again to call Tom. Still no answer. It was dinnertime, so I wasn't all that surprised that he wasn't there. I would try again a little later. Cell phones were something new at that time, and we hadn't yet decided that we had a need for one. At that moment I was thinking we had made the wrong decision. At least if he had one I could get in touch with him. Even if he could only talk for a minute I would at least know that he was okay. He was coming home the next afternoon, so I thought about what I would make for dinner. Maybe we would go out; although I was sure he would be ready to have a home cooked meal. So I decided to go to the store in the morning and get a roast to put in the slow cooker. He enjoyed that, and he loved to make cold roast beef sandwiches, so that would take care of lunches over the weekend. I made a shopping list, and found I was more relaxed now; taking my mind off the phone call was a good thing.

After I was done all that needed to be done around the house I was restless. I felt like I needed to get out, I hadn't left the house all week other than to walk the dogs. I needed some human contact, so I called Tom's sister and asked her if she wanted to go out for a drink. She said it was perfect timing. She needed to get out too. It had been snowing all week, so I guess no one had been out much. I changed my clothes, fixed up my hair, and was ready to head out. I was just about out the door when the phone rang. Hoping it was Tom I rushed back in before the answering machine picked up. It was Tom's cousin. She wanted to come along with Jan and me. The more the merrier, so I was off to pick up the ladies. We parked the car at my house, and walked the two blocks to the local pub. It was Thursday night, trivia night. We had tried to make the trivia night a regular thing, but life seemed to get in the way most of the time. Both of the girls had small children, so it wasn't as easy for them to just pick up and go. I was glad they were able to tonight. I needed the distraction. We found a table, and made sure we were entered in the trivia. We never won, but we always had a lot of fun playing. I thought again as we were sitting there how lucky I was to have them. From the beginning they had welcomed me into the family, and it had made moving so far away from my family easier. Right now I couldn't leave the country and go home because of the immigration process, but it was coming to an end. I had been granted a Green Card, and was just waiting for all the final documentation to come through. Then I could cross the border back into Canada, my home. Even though I had to revoke my citizenship to become a citizen in the United States, Canada would always be my home.

When trivia was over none of us were really ready to go home yet. We decided to stay for another drink, and then head out. We started talking, and filling each other in on what had gone on since we last talked, which in reality hadn't been all that long. But I sure had some news for them. I started to tell them about my phone call, and they were both in shock. They didn't understand how a mother could do that to her child. By the time I was done telling them everything that had gone on, including Tom's reaction to my search, the girls were in shock. They did agree with me that Tom would come around, they knew him as well as I did, so I trusted their opinions when it came to him.

The girls finally decided it was time to go home, and called for a cab. I waited with them until the cab got there, and then walked the couple blocks back home.

There is nothing better, in my opinion, than being greeted at the door by a dog. I had double the greetings, and was smothered in dog when I walked in the door. I always said that if your tension wasn't gone by the time they were done then there was something seriously wrong with you! Once I was able to get settled again I realized that Tom still hadn't called. Now I was worried. I looked at the clock, and it was still before 11 pm, so I decided it wasn't too late to call. No answer again. I left another message, and told him I was worried now, so please, please call and let me know you're okay. I thought I would likely hear from him soon. But I didn't. I spent a sleepless night, waking up with every noise, hoping it was the phone. It never was. In the morning I was so worried that before my feet hit the floor I was dialing the hotel. Still nothing, and I consoled myself by saying that maybe he had already checked out, and would be home later that day.

Chapter 6

I spent most of Friday working around the house, waiting for Tom to come home. I missed him more than usual, and I assumed it was because of the roller coaster I had been on this past week. As well as the fact that I hadn't been able to talk to him at all. That just wasn't normal for us. Maybe one day, but never more than that, had gone by without us talking, and I was very unsettled about it. I walked the dogs, started the roast, did laundry, cleaned the house, and then waited. I decided I would try to take my mind off Tom coming home by going back to the internet sites that I had found. I checked my email and there was one from my brother's wife. I got angry just seeing that it was there, and I hadn't even opened it yet! I took a deep breath, and opened it.

"Hey Emma

I hope you are doing okay with Tom away for the week. I haven't heard from you, so I assume you have been busy. I think it's great that you are going to search for your birth family. It hopefully will answer a lot of your questions, and hopefully they will be the answers you want to find. Keep me posted, and I want you to know that I am here if you need a confidante. Nothing you tell me will go any further.
I understand you not wanting to let a lot of people know, and you have my word I will not tell anyone.
Talk to you soon!

Linda"

I was furious when I finished reading the email. How dare she lie to me like that! Does she think that I don't know where Mom got her information from? Since she was the only person I had told at that time it was quite obvious who the leak was. Maybe she didn't know about the phone call. Chances are Mom would not have told her because it may put her in a different light, she wouldn't appear as perfect as she pretended to be. Even still, I was furious, and started to write a rather scathing email in reply. After typing for about five minutes I realized that maybe I was doing the wrong thing. I should either ignore her email, or act like everything was fine until I had the chance to confront her face to face. I did know that she would never hear another word from me about my search, or anything that I didn't want getting back to Mom for that matter. So I closed the email and deleted the reply. Then I opened up the sites that I had been to, and looked at the sites remaining on the list. I had been to about one third of them so far, so I started hitting some new ones.

After a couple of hours I was exhausted mentally. I just couldn't go to any more of these sites today. I needed a break from all the emotions this search was bringing up, and it was just the beginning. I knew that there was a lot more emotion to come. If I started getting responses to my search posts then I would have to be prepared for anything. It could be good news; it could be bad. Anything could happen from this point onwards.

I felt like I was done for the day, and needed a distraction again. It was mid-afternoon now, and I was hoping that Tom would pull in the driveway anytime. I grabbed a book and a beer and went to the window seat to relax.

About an hour later I looked up and saw Tom's car pulling in the driveway. I got butterflies all over again, it happened every time he came home, either from work or from a trip away. We were very happy and earlier that day I had had a phone call from the fertility clinic I had been referred to. They wanted to book an appointment. It was time they said; time to have a little help in trying to conceive. I had made the appointment for the next Friday, and just seeing him get out of the car it hit me: I could be pregnant by this time next week. It just dawned on me at that moment, and I fell in love with him all over again.

I ran out the door and raced the dogs to the car. I didn't get there first, which was normal. The dogs were so excited to see him, jumping, barking, whining, and one rolling onto her back for a belly rub. It was mayhem. And then I jumped right into the fray, wrapping my arms around my husband's neck and holding him so tight my arms hurt. We all headed for the house, the dogs running around and between us, almost tripping us. I loved this kind of chaos. It was a happy time for all of us. Once we were in the house and all calmed down I told Tom about the appointment the following week. I was the happiest I had ever been at that moment. My dreams were starting to come true. With any luck this time next year there would be a baby filling our lives with happiness. I wanted to remember this moment forever. I wished my mind had a compartment for pictures.

Then my life as I knew it fell apart.

Tom did not have the reaction I expected him to have. He wanted kids as much as I did, so why wasn't he as excited as me about this? We had been down a long road to get to this point, and all the tests that I had had to go through made the doctor feel confident that I would be able to get pregnant, and have a healthy pregnancy. I was confused, and a little hurt to be honest. I didn't get it.

I convinced myself that he was just taking it all in, and working through his own emotions. He had always been the more pragmatic one in our relationship, so I chalked it up to that and continued on with the day. I made dinner, and called Tom to come and eat. He came out to the kitchen and looked apprehensive. Again I fooled myself into thinking he was just tired from the drive today and the conference all week. So we ate dinner and chatted about anything and everything. That at least seemed normal. Tom was tired, so we decided we would just cuddle up on the couch and watch a movie. He let his family know he was home safe, and that he would talk to them over the weekend.

If I had only known that falling asleep that night in his arms was the last time that I would be this happy for a very long time I would have tried to find a way to stop time.

Chapter 7

On Saturday we had no plans. We hung around the house doing little things, but I could sense something was wrong with Tom. Over dinner I asked him if he had written any notes about my search. He said no, he hadn't had time. I asked him what he did all week, and he said work stuff. This Tom wasn't the Tom I knew and loved. He was sullen, and obviously had something on his mind. We had never had secrets before, and I didn't see any reason that we would start to now. During dinner I asked him what was bothering him, and he said he must just be tired from the week, and got up and left the table. Normally we would clean up together, and do dishes together. Not tonight. He left me sitting at the kitchen table, with all the clean up to do alone. I went to see where he was, and he was sitting in front of his computer. I tried to shrug it off, and went back to the kitchen to finish doing the dishes. All the time I was working away in the kitchen I couldn't shake the feeling that something was seriously wrong here. I just wish I knew what it was, but Tom wasn't letting me in. In all the time we had been together this had never happened. Now this just added to the stress I was already feeling about the search, and the fight with my Mom. I felt the tears rolling down my face, and I didn't try to stop them. Maybe a good cry would relieve some of the tension I was feeling.

When I was done cleaning up I made a cup of tea, and went to my window seat to stare into the darkness and gather my thoughts. I hadn't told him about the phone call from my Mom yet, it just hadn't seemed like the time since he had been home. So I knew that he wasn't upset about that, but that didn't mean he wasn't upset about my search. It was just after 7 p.m., and the dogs were restless. I decided that a walk would do us all good, and went to ask Tom if he wanted to go along.

"No Emma. I don't. I'm tired, and I just want to do what I want to do. Please let me," he replied.

Once again, I was dumbfounded. With tears in my eyes I got the dogs and myself ready and off we went. It was a warm winter night, and I was in no rush to go home again, so we took an extra long walk. The dogs were tired out when we got home, and I had decided that he wasn't going to shut me out any longer. We were going to talk about whatever it was that was bothering him.

I asked him to come out of the office and talk to me. Begrudgingly he did. I asked him if it was the fertility appointment that was bothering him. He sat silent. Finally I begged him to tell me what was going on with him. He took a deep breath, and gave me the most pained look I had ever seen on his face.

"Emma, this is eating me up. But I have to come clean before this appointment next Friday. More than anything I wanted to have kids with you. That just can't happen now."

I was crying again. "Tom, what is going on? You are really scaring me." I could hear my heart beating in my ears. Racing rather than beating.

Tom stood up, and with his back to me said, "I was not out of town just for work this week. I have met someone else, and it isn't the first time we have been together. You once asked me why wives never went on these trips, or why you had never met anyone from my office. Before I explain anymore to you, please let me say that I never meant to hurt you. We never meant to hurt you."

I sat there in disbelief, a scream blocked by the huge lump in my throat. Not my Tom, there's no way. We're in love. We're going to have a baby. He would never do this to me. He promised. Not just to me, but in front of God and all our witnesses in that church. Then it was like I just heard the last sentence that he had almost whispered. "We"? Why would some woman I don't know care if she was hurting me? I know her don't I? I couldn't make myself ask him.

I just looked at him. He looked so desperate. Like he wanted to console me, but there was no chance that I was going to let him anywhere near me. Not right now. Possibly not ever again. Finally I was able to whisper, "Who?"

He let out a wail like he was the one who was having his world ripped apart. He begged me not to ask him that.

I screamed at him, "Tell me who she is Tom! You at least owe me that much."

He cleared his throat, and he said, "Darlene."

My mind did not go to the Darlene that he meant. I thought it must be someone in his office. I knew the girl that answered the phones; her name was Sandra or something like that. Definitely not Darlene. I couldn't remember ever hearing that name before, other than, no, it couldn't be. "You mean Darlene who is still married to my foster brother? Oh god, no, it can't be her Tom. She's family. I'm wrong right?"

He just hung his head, and I could see him sob. I knew then that it was my foster brother's wife. They had separated a few months ago, and at the time I thought it happened rather quickly, but I just figured that no one can know all of what's going on in someone's marriage. If she ever wanted to talk about it, she knew I would listen. She had been calling us off and on over the last few months, but I just figured it was to have someone to talk to. Someone that wasn't right there in the middle of it all. I was so stupid! The thought that Tom would cheat on me had never once crossed my mind. I bet they both had a good laugh about it all. I steeled myself to ask more questions. I had to have more answers.

"Tom, I am so numb right now. I never thought this would be us. Not in a million years. But here we are, and while I'm numb, I still need some answers. I hope you will be honest with me, but I guess I will never truly know, will I? I didn't think you had ever lied to me right up until this very minute. I don't think these questions are going to be as hard for you to answer as they are for me to ask."

He looked at me with his sad eyes. I had only seen those eyes once before, maybe twice, but never in this kind of situation where I felt physically ill at the thought of consoling him. He sat down on the couch opposite me and said he would answer anything I asked.

"When did this start?" I asked.

"We started chatting online after the first time I met her when we went up to Canada for your parents' surprise wedding anniversary party. We chatted for a long time before she made the decision to leave Dale. I wanted to think that she didn't do it for me, but I think she did," he replied.

"Does Dale know?"

"No, she was going to tell him after this trip," he said, "and I was going to tell you at the same time. You just beat me to it. You have always been able to see into my heart, and know when there is something wrong."

"Oh stop Tom! Don't try to butter me up now. It's too late for that. Since the two of you planned to tell the two of us it was obviously not going to end. You and I were going to end. Right?"

"Emma, I don't know how I can ever make you understand this. I love you both. I truly do, but she gave me an ultimatum."

I scoffed at him. "She gave you what? An ultimatum? Since when does Tom do ultimatums? Do you even remember what you told me once about ultimatums? You don't do them. Your exact words. Now I find out that you do. And that this life we've had has all been a lie. I am so angry right now." And at that very moment a light bulb went off in my head. "Oh no Tom, please, do not tell me that everyone at your office thinks SHE is your wife?"

His face turned a little whiter, so I knew the answer. I was never invited to the conferences or to anything at his office because he was taking his "other" wife. He just made a huge fool out of me and an even bigger sham of our marriage by taking her and passing her off as me. I wanted to know if they knew her as Emma too but I couldn't bear to ask. I just sat there, holding one of the dogs, staring out the window. I couldn't move. I felt like I was paralyzed, and didn't know what I would do if I did get up anyway.

After about five minutes, which felt more like five hours, I heard him walk out of the room towards the office. I called him back, and I told him that I wanted to know if she had told my brother yet. He said he doubted it, because she hadn't gone home yet. She had come back to town with him and was in a hotel room. I just looked at him. I couldn't believe what I was hearing.

"I assume Dale has the kids right? He has had them all week?"

"Yes, he does," he replied. "Darlene isn't going home until at least Monday."

"Do not even say her name in front of me!" I spat at him.

He apologized. It meant nothing to me at all. I would never have believed that I could feel this way about Tom, and so quickly. I can't say it was hatred, but it was an intense dislike, whereas an hour ago I was dreaming about our future, and our baby that could be on the way soon. That dream was now gone. I can forgive a lot of things, but not this. This kind of betrayal cuts too deep, and hurts too much to ever be repaired, and if I couldn't wholly give myself to anyone, I couldn't be with that person. Tom knew this before he entered into any kind of relationship with my sister-in-law. We had talked about things like that during our time together. I thought he felt the same way as me. I told him that if I ever felt I wanted to be with someone else, I would tell him before it happened, so as to spare him some dignity, and possibly some hurt. He never gave me that opportunity. He just betrayed everything he said he would never do to me. It proved to me that he didn't want our marriage to be saved. He wanted out. And he was going to be able to walk away, because I would not beg him to stay. He was free to go start his new life. But with my sister-in-law? Really?

I focused again on what he was saying. Wait a minute! She's here. In a hotel room. This just gets better and better.

"I guess I should feel honoured that you came home last night and slept in our bed with me?" I said sarcastically.

He just sighed.

I walked over to the kitchen table and grabbed the phone. I pushed the speed dial button for my brother's house. It rang three times, and just as I was going to hang up he answered. He sounded out of breath, and then I realized he was probably putting the kids to bed. I tried to sound as cheery as I could, and asked him if he was busy. He said he was, but he would call me right back. Just give him a few minutes to put the kids down.

So I waited.

Tom asked me what I was going to tell Dale. I told him he did not have the right to ask me anything anymore. Unless it was how much money I needed. Being in a foreign country, and not having my green card yet, I had no source of income. I hoped that he knew he was going to continue to support me until I decided what I was going to do with my life now, and had the means to support myself. I did tell him that he was going to be in the room with me when Dale called. I wanted him to hear what I had to say. What he didn't know was that I was going to make him tell Dale. Why should I have to do it? Dale was still so much in love with his wife, and still had high hopes of reconciling with her. Obviously she had been just as honest with him as Tom had been with me. I was furious, and I was not going to be the one to rip my brother's heart out.

While we waited for Dale to call back I was able to gather enough presence of mind together to think logically about this whole situation. I told him he could repack his bag while we waited, and when we got off the phone with Dale he could leave. It wasn't a question; it was what was going to happen. I told him he would not uproot me and the dogs, just to have his new lover sleep in my bed. As well as him leaving, he would make sure that she was footing the hotel bill. I needed to be able to live, and I would be damned if she was going to use money that I needed to live in a hotel room with my husband.

He was very conciliatory. He knew not to question me, and I think he maybe even saw the "fairness" in it, if that was a word that could be used in this situation.

Dale called back about thirty minutes later, and the first thing he asked was what was wrong? He could tell I had been crying, just by the sound of my voice. I put him on speaker phone, and told him that Tom would explain it all to him. Tom begged me with his eyes not to make him do it, but I just set the phone on the coffee table and turned my head from him. Dale was concerned, as he had every right to be.

Tom told him everything; at least he told him what he had told me. I would never know if that was the whole story or not, and at that point I didn't want to know anymore. I knew enough to know that my world had just fallen apart. That was enough.

Dale couldn't speak. He was breathing heavy, and I couldn't tell if he was crying, or so mad that he wanted to crawl through the phone line and strangle Tom. I wouldn't blame him for either. Tom had very carefully made sure not to mention the hotel that Darlene was in, and I'm sure that was to keep it from me as well.

Dale reassured me that he was okay enough to get through the night, and he made me assure him that I was as well. I knew I could get through anything, I had before, and there's really no other choice, right? I would triumph over this, one way or another. Sure, I was going to be angry and sad, and every other emotion I could think of, for a while, but eventually I would get over it. Well, maybe not over it, I don't think I could ever truly be over it, but I would move past it and forge a new life for myself. I was like a phoenix rising from the ashes. A stronger version of myself would emerge out the other end of this. I just didn't know this at the time. At the time I was just crushed and vulnerable.

We hung up, after saying that we would talk tomorrow, and I walked out of the room.

I couldn't look at Tom. I couldn't even be near him. To be honest, I didn't want him in the same house. When he walked into the bedroom I told him as much, and he quietly packed and walked out. I hollered after him to leave his house keys, he would have no use for them anymore, at least not as long as I was here. He started to object, and then decided better of it, leaving his keys on the kitchen table as he left. Hearing his car drive away, knowing he was going to the arms of another woman, nearly broke me. I sobbed so hard I could barely catch my breath. The dogs came to comfort me, and we all curled up on the bed, me sobbing, them cuddling up to me, trying to make me feel better.

I guess I finally cried myself to sleep, and when I woke up it was 2 a.m. I got up, changed into my pajamas, locked up the house and crawled back into bed. I was so exhausted that I barely remembered doing any of it. When I woke again it was Sunday morning.

Chapter 8

Sunday morning I woke up earlier than normal, and for one precious moment I didn't remember all that had happened the night before. I looked over and Tom's side of the bed was empty. I thought, for one split second, that he was up, having coffee and reading the Sunday paper already, and then it all came back to me. I was alone, not just in bed, but in life. I had been alone before, after my first marriage, and I was okay with being alone. I didn't want to be alone though. I wanted Tom. I wanted my husband. But that was never going to happen again.

I dragged myself out of bed, turned on the coffee, and stood under a hot shower until I felt more awake. I got dressed, and headed for the kitchen to get coffee. Coffee always started my day off right. I liked to have my first cup in silence. After that I was ready to begin the day. Today was different though. The old routine was gone, and I was left to pick up the pieces of my life, and figure out where I was going from here. It was too much for me to think about right then.

I got the dogs ready to go, and we went for a long walk. It was another sunny, warm winter day, and we didn't rush home because there was nothing there to go home to. So we walked and played in the snow, and I thought about my new life. What would I do? I knew I would move back to Canada, but when? Would I move back to the area my family was in, or start somewhere new? So many things had to be decided, but I needed time to make sure I was making the right decisions.

When we were almost home again it dawned on me that Tom would more than likely end up moving to Canada now too. He would never do it for me, but, my brother was not going to allow his children to be taken out of the country. At least I hoped he wouldn't, and I would be sure to have a conversation with him about it sometime in the near future. I felt so bad for him. His world had just crashed again for the second time in a few months. He would know now that there was no hope of reconciliation for him and Darlene. There were also two children, one four years old, the other just a toddler at eighteen months. This was going to affect them as well. It made my life seem simple in comparison to his.

I couldn't get past the thought that Tom would, in all likelihood, move to Canada at some point in the future. Before we were married there was not even the chance of discussing him moving. It would never happen, he was born in the United States, and the United States is where he would be living out his life. But now the tables had turned. He would have to move there if they wanted to be together. He also got his instant family. I wondered if they would have children together.

I had to put it out of my mind. I couldn't continue to think about what they would do. The pressing issue was what I would do. I would be moving back to Canada, without a doubt, and that move would have to happen relatively soon. I just had to decide where I would move to. Somewhere familiar or somewhere new? Both had their good points and their bad. For the time being I felt settled enough with knowing I would move back to Canada. The rest would follow at the right time.

I poured another cup of coffee and took it to my window seat. It's funny the things that go through your mind at a time like this. I thought about how much I would miss this seat, and it made me sad all over again. I moved to the office, hoping to leave that sadness on the window seat for a while. I turned on my computer and checked my email. There was nothing really important to deal with. So I moved to the internet, and checked the sites I had registered at to see if there had been any replies. Nothing there either.

Now what do I do with myself? I felt lost again, and I didn't want to give into these feelings. I realized I was going to have to tell my Mom what was going on, but that could wait for another day. With any luck maybe Dale would beat me to it, because I knew that Mom would turn it all around to be my fault somehow. If she did I knew it would be the final straw, and I didn't think that our relationship would be able to be repaired if that happened. This was not my fault, in any way. I knew that. Dale knew that. If Tom was honest with his family then they would know it too. But that was between his conscience and his family. I couldn't face them right now.

Just as I was thinking this the phone rang. It was Tom's sister. I let it go to the answering machine. I could avoid her for a day or two, and if Tom had not told his family by then, I would. It stands to reason that they would support him, and I expected no less. I really had no hope of continuing my friendships with his family. Once I was gone I would not want to know what he was doing, and it would be hard enough knowing that he was still linked to my family. I laughed to myself and thought to myself that my husband isn't my grandfather, but, he is likely to be my niece and nephew's step-father. I wonder what that would make him to me. I guess just my ex-husband, but in time I was sure I would find some kind of humour in it.

The rest of the day I spent trying to occupy my mind with anything but Tom. It was not as easy as it would seem to be. There was nothing on TV that I wanted to watch, or that could hold my interest. I couldn't concentrate on my book, and found myself reading the same pages over and over. I brushed both dogs, and played with them. I could tell they were waiting for Tom to come home again. They didn't understand why he went away again last night, or why he wasn't here now. It hurt me to know that I couldn't explain it to them, so I had to make sure to give them extra attention in the coming days and weeks, until I felt like they had adjusted to this new life. It was a long day, but eventually it was bedtime, and I was able to put this day behind me. My last thought before I went to sleep was that I made it through day one, and I can make it through this one day at a time.

Chapter 9

Monday was a better day than Sunday, which made me feel a little stronger. I needed that strength to draw on when Tom called in the afternoon. He wanted to meet somewhere so we could talk. I told him to come to the house, not home, but to the house, because the dogs missed him, and they needed a chance to see him. He said he would be over after work, and offered to bring dinner. I didn't want him doing anything for me, but I had to eat right? He brought pizza and beer.

We sat at the table, avoiding eye contact with each other, and eating in silence. The silence was deafening. Finally when I couldn't take it anymore I asked him what it was that he wanted to say to me.

Tom started by saying that he was worried about me.

I told him he gave up that right when he cheated on me. "You don't get to worry about me anymore Tom. You made the choice, and now you have to live with it. Whether I am doing okay or not is, frankly, none of your business now."

He hung his head. He knew I was right. There was not going to be any friendship, or friendly parting of ways. If he had been honest with me from the very day he realized he was starting to have feelings for another woman, maybe friendship would have been a possibility somewhere down the road. But not now. He had ruined any chance there was of me ever trusting him again.

There is a saying that rings true now. "If you love two people, pick the second one, because you never really loved the first one." I am the first one unfortunately. Darlene is the second one. She got the man. She stole my family. There is no forgiving. No forgetting. At least not for me.

I told him that I would be moving back to Canada soon. We needed to come up with a plan for that to happen. I didn't have to like him right now, but he was darn well going to help me get out of here, and into a new place. Not just monetarily, but physically as well. I knew deep down that I was not going to be able to count on any family support. Mom would be sure of that. What she said was the law in our family, and if she told my brothers and my sister that they need not have anything to do with me anymore, then that is what would happen. That much I knew was true.

He asked me where I was going to move to, and I told him I didn't know yet. I hadn't thought that far ahead yet, and then I got mad. Why did he want me out and gone so quickly? I felt like the two of them had already made all their plans, and in that plan there was me. They had decided what I would do and when I would do it.

Now I was furious. He would not have any control over my life from this point on. I would make my own decisions, and I would inform him what those decisions were when and if they concerned him.

Clearly we were not ready to have a civil conversation yet, but Tom had one more thing to ask of me. How he had the nerve to ask me this I couldn't fathom. He wanted to stay here starting Wednesday night. He wanted to what? I couldn't believe what I was hearing. His new girlfriend was going back home Wednesday morning, so he didn't see the point in staying in the hotel.

Well I sure did, and I told him as much. He asked me to think about it. I just shook my head and laughed, then asked him to get what he needed, and leave. I had said all I wanted to right now, and I wanted to be alone. We could try talking another day, sometime in the future.

Tom packed more clothes, leaving his dirty laundry, probably hoping I would do it for him. Not a chance! I was not feeling the need to do anything for him. So his laundry would sit until he figured out what to do with it.

When he finally left, I felt completely exhausted. I decided to have another hot shower and wash the day off me, then go to bed early. Tuesday would be a better day. It had to be. I would make it a better day.

Chapter 10

Tuesday did start out to be a better day. I was calmer, and I felt like my mind was not as muddled. I was able to concentrate on things, and actually think some things through. I made some decisions, the biggest being that I would be moving back to the city where I went to college. I knew there would be a lot of changes since I had been there, but, there would also still be many things the same. I knew that I could make a go of it on my own there. I may be shattered right now, but each day would see a tiny crack heal, day by day until I was whole again. Being in a familiar city, and new place, would help that process along. Memories of my life with Tom wouldn't be triggered everywhere I looked. It was a start. A new beginning. I was looking forward to it in some ways, starting to feel a little excited even.

Making that decision led me to the classified ads online in London. I needed somewhere to live. I emailed any place I could making inquiries about information on rentals. I had emailed at least ten places, and decided that was enough for one day.

I did some cleaning, and laundry, and made myself a dinner of munchies. Carrots, celery, cauliflower, ranch dip, and a small plate of nachos with cheese. I ate in front of the TV, and I didn't jump up to do the dishes immediately after I ate. There was no one to notice the mess but me, so I didn't feel the need to rush. Essentially I tried to do anything that wasn't part of the normal routine, hoping that I wouldn't be constantly thinking about what wasn't there any longer. Of course it was difficult not to miss Tom, he did live here with me, and mostly everything of his was still here.

I decided late in the evening that I had to do one thing before I went to bed. I had to take down all the pictures of us, so that I wouldn't constantly be seeing his face everywhere I looked. I went to the basement to find a box, and looked around. I suddenly had a solution to Tom wanting to stay here. There was a pull out couch in the basement, as well as another room where he could put his computer if he wanted until I was gone. I pulled out the sofa bed, and threw on some sheets and a blanket. I cleaned up the area a little, and then brought down his things from his nightstand. There. Perfect. He had his own little space, and would not be bothered by me. I really only needed to go down there to do laundry, and I could do my laundry during the day. I could also fill boxes during the day so that I wasn't disturbing him. The last thing I did was take the second phone downstairs and hook it up for him. I was proud of myself that I was able to do all that for him, and not just throw all his stuff down the steps.

I finished up for the night and went to bed, alone, wondering if I could ever get used to not having him in bed beside me.

Chapter 11

Tom called me Wednesday morning to see if I was ready to talk to him again. I told him that he could come home starting that night, but he would have his own separate living space in the basement. If that wasn't acceptable to him then he would have to make other arrangements on his own. He thought that would work for him and said he would be there later that day. He also said he would make dinner for me. I was too worn down to fight about it and let it go at that. When I hung up the phone I realized that, even though in my heart he was the love of my life, my mind had stepped in and protected me from that hurt, and got me through the first civil conversation we had had since he told me his news.

I spent the rest of the day searching for a place to live in London. I had not found anything that seemed suitable to me yet, and I started to wonder if I should just take the cheapest one available and then search for something more desirable when I was settled. As I worked around the house I thought about it, and decided that it was the best option. Of course I wasn't going to take a place in an area that wasn't safe, and I hoped that the people searching for me would take that into consideration. I went back to my computer and emailed the people searching for me, adding that I was willing to take the first available, providing it was in a safe area, and was a reasonable price.

Tom was going to have to help me out with rent until I was on my feet and had some kind of income. I would take any work I could when I got there, going on the same premise as finding a place. As long as I have a job I can search for another one that might be better suited to me.

I felt pretty good about things, and wrote a note to myself of things to go over with Tom when he came home later that day.

1.   Decide on amount of rent he can afford.

2.   We will have to go through everything in the house and agree on who gets what.

3.   Divorce proceedings? To save money, if we can do this amicably, I would be willing to use the same legal representation.

4.   We need to set some boundaries where my family is concerned – Tom will still be peripherally involved with everyone, and we need to set some kind of boundary.

5.   Moving date and Tom's role in that.

6.   House rules here re: meals, entertainment, etc.

I felt these were the main items for me that needed to be settled. It wouldn't be anything concrete, or even written down. It's sad that we would even have to have a conversation like that, but it had to be done. Things had changed, and nothing could be taken for granted anymore between us. I marveled at how a person's security and sense of self can be shattered in an instant.

I realized then that I would have to start packing up all my clothes and personal items, and figured there was no time like the present to begin. I went down to the basement and carried up what boxes I could manage to gather. First I started with photo albums and books. The books were easy. There was really nothing that he and I had in common when it came to reading. I read a lot, as much as I could, and he rarely read. When he did read it was war stories, and military books. Once I had some boxes packed I had to find a place for them. The office closet seemed like the best place, so I carried them in there. I sat at my desk to take a small break and there sat my Adoption Order. It seemed like a long time ago since I had even thought about it, but it had only been a few days. Beside that piece of paper, on another piece of paper, I had written down the appointment time for this Friday, and had doodled little pink and blue balloons and bows. Looking at that reminded me that I would no longer need the appointment, and how much had changed. Just a few days ago my biggest worry was if the procedure would work, and how excited we both would be to be parents. I started to shake, and the tears once again poured out of me. It was like a tap had been turned on. I couldn't breathe, and I couldn't move. My biggest dream, along with every other dream I had, had been popped, just like those tiny blue and pink balloons, by my husband. The man that was supposed to love me and protect me from any kind of hurt.

When I stopped sobbing, and was finally able to breathe again, I felt the anger building once more. The lies that he told me. The lies that SHE had told me. It all came flooding back, and I was enraged. I wanted to throw something. I wanted to hurt him as bad as he had hurt me. And at that instant he walked through the door. I ran at him, fists flying, insults hurtling through the air. He stopped me, and held me by my arms, and yelled at me to stop. Me? Why did I have to stop? I was not the one that had caused any of this! I guess he thought I had started to calm down, when it was really the shock I felt over his nerve to tell me to stop. I slapped him across the face hard; with every ounce of power I had in me, and called him a selfish bastard. I told him to get out, and not come back. He turned and left, head down, like a little boy who had been caught with his hand in the cookie jar.

But suddenly I felt better. I felt like I was on top for once in this situation. And it felt good!

I turned around and locked the door, and I did not see him again until the day I moved out.

Chapter 12

The rest of that week I spent packing up what I could, looking for a place to start my life over, and dealing with practical issues.

The first thing I had to do was cancel the Friday appointment. I couldn't leave it hanging. After discovering the piece of paper the day before I hadn't stopped thinking about it, and how I would explain the cancellation. In the end I decided what I would do. I called them as soon as they opened on Thursday. When the receptionist answered I told her that I had to cancel an appointment for the next day. She cancelled the appointment and then asked me if I wanted to reschedule. I said no, that I would not be going through with the procedure because my husband had found a new girlfriend. During the ensuing silence I felt horrible. It wasn't her fault that my husband was such an ass. He knew when this whole infertility roller coaster started that he was with someone else, and I was guessing that by that time he knew what he was going to do. He was going to rip my heart out and stomp on it. He was not going to stay with me, and that made me even more furious. But in the meantime I needed to apologize to this poor girl on the other end of the phone line. I told her how sorry I was, that I couldn't apologize enough for my behaviour. I hoped she would forgive me. She said it was no problem, I should just forget it. I couldn't forget it, and as soon as we were off the phone I called and ordered flowers and chocolates for her specifically, and a fruit basket for the whole office, to thank them for everything they had done for me, and, again, to apologize to the receptionist. I used Tom's credit card. That gave me a sense of satisfaction that had me on a high for hours that day. Every time I thought about it, I laughed, and was really kind of proud of myself for coming up with that little bit of revenge so quickly. It was not in my nature to be diabolical, but, surprisingly, it felt good!

Dale called me that afternoon. He sounded defeated; as I'm sure I did to him as well. Darlene had come to pick up the kids on Wednesday, and apparently she was very contrite. By the time Dale told me what he had been told it was obvious to me that my husband and his wife had come up with a scripted version of what the two of us were going to know. He was so sad. But he did say it wasn't for him, it was for the kids. He had some time alone with the knowledge of what had been going on before she finally confessed to him, so he was prepared. He knew what he wanted to say to her, and knew as well what he was going to tell his lawyer. Darlene was not going to make out as well as she thought in the divorce. He was certainly going to use the adultery against her any way he could, and I was proud of him for doing it. He had come to the same conclusions that I had. Tom was going to have to move to Canada if they wanted to be together, and he was not going to let his children be around him if he could help it. He was going to fight for sole custody, which was probably not going to happen with the way custody battles go nowadays, but he was hoping that she would only get weekend visits, and some holidays. I told him how proud I was of him and that if I could help at all with his case I would. After all, who knew Tom better, right?

We chatted about other things for a few minutes, mostly how the kids were doing, and then the other shoe dropped. Dale had talked to Mom about it all, and, as I had figured, Mom blamed me for pushing Tom away, towards Darlene. Part of me was shocked, but the part of me that wasn't shocked just laughed out loud. I knew now for sure that the fracture had become a complete break, and that I would never be welcome in my Mom's life again. I knew I could make it without her, but it was still very hurtful at the time. What mother turns her back on her child, blood or not? To me it just further proved to me that she didn't want me. Eventually I would come to the conclusion that it was her loss because I wasn't a bad person. It took a long time though. Again it was mind over heart, and those reconciliations don't come easy.

Brenda Seymour

Later that day I checked my email, and there was a reply from an agent that had found a place for me. I knew the area having lived in the city. I knew it wasn't the greatest area, but there were worse areas as well. Maybe the area had changed since I lived there and I might really like it. If not there was always the option to move once I had the means to. I emailed her back and told her I would take it. The available date was January first. A new year. A new place. A new start. Maybe it was a sign.

That left about six weeks to get everything done, plenty of time for me to be ready to go. This part of my life was going to be left behind me, and with any luck a lot of the sorrow and heart ache that I felt would be left with it.

I emailed Tom with the details, and told him what I expected of him. It was not a negotiation, if he was half the man he said he was he would do this, and support me until I was on my feet. Surprisingly, I had a reply in what seemed like seconds. He said he would do whatever I wanted him to do, and my first thought was that there's something else he doesn't want me to find out, so he was going along with it hoping that his agreeing with me would keep me from digging. I wasn't going digging for anything more, I had had enough of his crap to last a lifetime. I was, however, planning a little revenge, purely for my own entertainment.

Chapter 13

I decided that Friday was going to be a "me" day. I was not going to think about Tom. I was going to focus on me and the new life that I was about to start. I spent extra time with the dogs because they were out of sorts. They didn't know what was going on, and how could I explain it to them? I tried to put them at ease as much as I could, and later in the day they seemed more relaxed, and in better spirits. Seeing them so relaxed made me feel better, so I curled up on the window seat with them, and for the first time in days I had a cup of tea, read my book, and actually felt a lot of the stress leave my body. I wanted this feeling to last, so I locked the doors and turned off the phones. This weekend was going to be my own little retreat. Anyone that wanted to talk to me, or needed to talk to me, was going to have to wait until at least Monday. In my opinion, at that point, answering machines were the best thing ever. I was even going to ignore any emails that I saw from people I didn't want to interact with. I was going to recharge myself, body and soul.

By Monday morning I was feeling much better about my plans, and I was going to cement everything this week if I could. I had to make the arrangements to get a moving truck, and called around to find the best price. Being Christmas time most companies had great availability, and I actually ended up hiring a company that would come and load the truck, drive it to Ontario, and unload it. All on Tom's dime, of course. By doing this I was able to get around having to have him help me with the move, and not having to see him was worth the extra money. I sent Tom an email with the details, dates, times, and costs, which of course had already been put on hold on his credit card. This meant that it was time for me to find out from him what he wanted, and how close his list was to mine. As it turned out there weren't many items that we were going to have to make decisions on. In fact there were some things that neither of us really wanted, which meant that he was getting them.

I was the one doing the packing after all, and what I didn't want wasn't getting packed. A lot of the things we had two of, some better than others, but Tom wasn't really putting up a fight for much. That surprised me until I thought about it. He knew what Darlene already had, so why would he need the same things from our house? It all turned out to my benefit in the end, even though I was actually trying to be fair to him. With the division of all our belongings done I was able to pack most everything else up. I kept out the things I thought I would need for the next few weeks, just like anyone would normally do for a move. Again I was actually feeling pretty good about the progress of things.

On Friday I received another email from Tom. He wanted to come and get a few things from the house, if I would let him. I was feeling pretty good about things by then, and said he could come that night. As long as he didn't try to take anything out of here that we had agreed was going with me, I had no problem with it. In fact, I planned to stay as far away from him as I could while he was here. There was nothing left to say, and too many hurt feelings to be cordial.

He showed up just after dinner, and grabbed more clothes, his computer, and a few other necessities. I didn't ask him where he was staying because as long as it wasn't here I didn't really care. He left a key lying on the kitchen table, quite conspicuously actually, which was from a local motel. I felt no sympathy for him, and I was not going to be baited by it. Knowing him the way I did I knew that he laid it there knowing I would see it, and more than likely was hoping to spark some kind of response. It didn't work. I had a few secrets up my sleeve that he didn't know about, and they gave me a warm and fuzzy feeling while he was there. He would find out in due time of course what they were, but by then I would be out of the house, and wouldn't terribly care what happened here.

After he left I cleaned up the mess he had left behind and took a long bath with a tall glass of wine. It was my treat to myself, as I had realized that the only person I truly could count on was me, so I was the only one that I could count on to treat myself to the little things. The dogs and I curled up in bed and watched movies the rest of the evening, and woke up Saturday morning feeling quite refreshed.

The weather was quite nice for November, so I decided I would take the dogs out to the beach one last time before I moved. Unfortunately I was going to have to leave them behind when I moved because I couldn't have pets, and that broke my heart more than anything, so I tried not to think about it. Tom would keep the dogs, and I made him promise me that if he ever had to get rid of them that he would contact me first, because I would want them with me if I could have them. I found out later he didn't keep that promise either. I suppose I should have known better than to trust him on anything, but I thought he would at least keep that one. To this day I miss them, and I hope that they are loved, wherever they are. They were such good dogs that I am sure they are being spoiled where they are now. I have to believe that, or I would make myself crazy with worry over them. So that weekend I devoted myself to them, to making them happy, so that I would have some wonderful memories of them. There were a lot of tears shed, and even more pictures taken. They would forever hold a spot in my heart that could not be replaced by anything or anyone.

Chapter 14

The next few weeks were spent keeping myself busy. I never heard from Tom's sister or cousin again, and that surprised me a little. But, they were his family, and one thing his family did was stick together. Right or wrong. I gave them credit for standing with him, but I did wonder sometimes what story they knew. It wasn't my concern anymore, they had made the decision for themselves to cease contact and essentially end our friendships. Losing friends always hurts, but, I had never had a lot of true friends because I was scared to let people in. I had two friends that I could count on, no matter what was going on in my life, and they were the ones I counted on now. What I didn't know was that they had gone to the agent that I had dealt with to get the apartment, and told her the whole story. The agent let them have a key since it was empty for a couple of weeks before I was moving in. Technically it was still the former renters place, but the agent arranged with them to let my girls in to do what they do best. When I got there with the moving truck my apartment had been cleaned top to bottom, my refrigerator had been stocked with my favourite things, and any furniture that I had left with Tom had been supplied by my best friends. I was in total amazement over what they had done. They had not only cleaned, but painted as well. There was a beautiful bouquet of flowers on the kitchen table, with a note that the wine was in the fridge, along with my favourite picture of the three of us in a frame that said "Best Friends Live in Each Other's Hearts". I cried seeing all they had done for me, and then laughed when they walked in the door carrying boxes. I hadn't seen them in over a year because of the green card proceedings, and they hadn't been able to travel down to see me. It was so wonderful to be home, and I knew I was home because they were there with me. We spent that day talking and laughing and moving things around. We were tired by dinner time, but decided we were going out anyway. So I found some decent jeans and a t-shirt, and off we went. It ended up being just what I needed. We went to a pub that we had frequented in college, and talked about old times, and the new times that were to come. That night was the most fun I had had in a long time, and when we got back to my new place they had yet another surprise for me. I was a little confused at first when they got out of the car with me, until I saw what they were getting out of the trunk. Sleeping bags. We were having a sleep over! I was so excited, and so grateful to them for not making me spend my first night alone in the new place. I was missing my dogs, and being alone, totally alone, in a new place was a little scary and made me sad. We sat up till the wee hours of the morning, and finally collapsed into sleep sometime around 4 a.m.

The next day they helped me finish unpacking everything. We got rid of all the boxes and cleaned the place up. Standing arm in arm with each other and looking around the place made us all smile. There was a lot of me, and a little of both of them in my new place. I felt blessed, and I was confident that I was going to make it here. I had to. There was no other choice.

Saturday afternoon the girls left, and I was alone for the first time. I looked at what I knew would be my favourite spot in the apartment, made myself a cup of tea, and curled up on the window seat of the bay window. I was on the ground floor of a century old house, and I was already in love with the place. It was the window seat. That made it home for me. I sat there looking out the window, taking in the neighbourhood, and realized for the first time that the neighbourhood had certainly changed since I lived in the city. The changes were good. It was a middle class neighbourhood, and so far it seemed to be a quiet street. The truth would come out in the summer, when people were outside more. It didn't matter to me though, I wasn't moving, not unless I could take my window seat with me. My friends had dressed the window seat up for me, knowing that I would spend hours there. There were pillows, and even a small lap blanket to wrap up in. Beside the window was a small telephone table, with everything I would need while I was sitting there. Writing paper, a phone, and a small shelf with a few of my favourite books on it. I was so blessed to have my friends, and I decided then that I would do something great for them to thank them. I didn't know what yet, but I would come up with something. Considering what brought me back here, it was starting to dawn on me that I should have been here all along.

I spent Sunday puttering around the apartment, and it was a nice sunny day so I took a walk around the neighbourhood. The more I saw of it the more I liked it. Houses were well taken care of. Most homes looked like family homes. I was certain I would stay here for a long time.

Sunday evening I turned on my computer planning to plot a course of action for the week. It was not the greatest time of the year to be job hunting, but finding a job was my first priority. While I knew that Tom had agreed to support me the sooner I was making my own money, and not relying on his, the better. I wanted to show him I could make it without him, even though I didn't have to prove anything to him. I owed him nothing, and the sooner that tie was cut, the easier it would be for me to move on.

I found some local websites with employment opportunities, and bookmarked them. Monday morning, first thing, I would be back on those sites to start my job hunt. I also looked up the address of the local employment office, and other local agencies that helped people looking for work. I had spent a couple of hours looking, and decided it was enough to get me going. Then I decided I would check my email. There was one from the rental agent welcoming me, and letting me know to contact her with any issues I might have. I sent her a short reply saying that I couldn't thank her enough for all of her help, and that right now there were no problems at all. I was content here, and being content was a great feeling. I made a note to send her flowers or a fruit basket in the coming week. While I was hunting around on my desk for a notepad

I came across a pile of papers that I decided I should take a look through and clean the pile up. The first few things were contracts for the moving company, and papers from the rental company, along with a copy of my lease. I filed them away, and turned back to the pile. Right on top was my Adoption Order. I held it in my hand, and got lost in thought. Wondering and hoping for a happy ending to my search, which I planned to get back to right as soon as I had a job. I hoped that wouldn't be too far in the future. Soon after I shut everything down, made sure my doors were locked, and curled up on the couch to watch a movie before I went to bed. Little by little I felt all the stress of the breakup leaving me. It was a good feeling. I slept like a baby that night.

Chapter 15

Monday morning when I woke up I had mixed emotions. I felt very alone, but at the same time I felt liberated. I turned on the coffee maker, and went to have a shower. Standing under the hot water I tried to clear the cobwebs, and get my mind focused. I had my plan for the day, and I focused on that, partly because I needed a job, and partly because I didn't want to think about Tom, or my adoption search, or my family. In order to get a job I needed to have a positive attitude, and thinking about anything but the job search didn't leave me in a positive frame of mind.

After having my shower and getting dressed in some comfy clothes I made a coffee and turned my computer on. While it was warming up I had a bowl of cereal, and cleaned up the kitchen. It was nice to not have anyone other than myself to clean up after, but I did miss my dogs. I would always miss them, hopefully less and less as time went on.

I sat down at my computer and took a deep breath. My new life was starting now, and as much as I was glad to be where I was, it was a little scary too. I never thought I would be alone at 32, and starting over, but here I was. I took a look at my resume, made some updates, and started sending them out via email to as many places as I could. I still planned to take the first thing that came up, and if it wasn't really the job I wanted, then I would continue to look in my off time. There was an ad for a part time clerk needed at a bookstore. Now THAT would be my dream job, but I didn't think part time would be enough. I sent off my resume anyway, and after I printed the posting out I put a star on it, and started a new pile for jobs I really wanted to follow up on. After a couple of hours I had applied to over 25 places, and felt that I had made a great start. If I could do this every day then I might have a job before long. I crossed my fingers and hoped. I decided that I would head out to the Employment Office next, so I found the address again, and made sure I knew where it was. I was off, resumes in hand, and prepared to do what it took. I made it there, and spoke to a woman about my situation, only to find out that I could have done this all from home. I went back home, and went through their job bank online, and found six or seven more positions to apply for. One of the jobs was at an Answering Service. I didn't really even know what an answering service was, but for some reason that job stuck in my mind. I went through the pile of postings I had again, and pulled that one out and put it with the ad for the bookstore. It was lunchtime now, so I had some yogurt and an apple, and thought about what I was going to do for the rest of the day. I decided I would make a cup of tea and sit in the window and read for a while.

Sitting there trying to read my book I spotted the copy of my adoption order that I had tacked up on the bulletin board by my computer desk. Staring at it I decided that there was no time like the present to start my search. I finished my tea, and read my book for a while longer, and then I moved back to my computer. I keyed in "adoption search Ontario" in Bing and again came up with so many sites that it was kind of overwhelming. But, all I could do is start with the first one and move through them. A lot of the sites were sites to enter my information so that others could contact me if they were looking, and I filled out as many of those as I could. One of the search sites I found was called CanAdopt. There was a lot of information on this site; it was more than just a registry. There were mailing lists to join as well, and since I was new to this I signed up for them all. In time I would thin that list out to just a few of the topics. The week that I was getting ready to move I had sent a request to the Adoption Disclosure Registry, which would send me any information they had about my birth mother or birth father, so I didn't have much information to register on this site, other than what my adoption order gave me. I would be waiting for a while I was sure for the information from the government. But in the meantime I had a little information, and I felt lucky for that. Many people had no information, other than what they had been told by their adoptive families, and in my experience, most of the time that wasn't much.

I looked at the clock and was surprised to realize that I had been sitting there for almost four hours. I got up and moved around, and decided that my mind was so overloaded right now, and my body was sore from sitting, so I needed a walk to clear my mind, and stretch my body out. I bundled up as it was snowing lightly. Not too heavy to go out in, but enough that I needed to bundle up. I enjoyed the walk, seeing more people out in the neighbourhood, and felt refreshed when I got back home. I made some dinner, and settled in for the evening to watch a movie or some TV before bedtime. I flipped through the channels and couldn't find anything that captured my attention, so I turned the TV off and went back to my computer for a while. I had a lot of email to go through all of a sudden; there was just a flood from the search site I had joined that had the email lists. I was shocked at the number of people who had responded to my information; most welcoming me to the group, and a few that were offering to help if they could. There was one from a woman in British Columbia that caught my eye. She seemed genuine, and asked me for more information. I responded, telling her that right now I didn't have any more information than I had posted, but I would post more as I got it. I did remember being told when I was younger that my mother had been in Toronto, but was really from Newfoundland. That was all I knew, and I didn't really know that the Newfoundland connection was accurate. I shut my computer down for the night, and tried to watch some TV. Eventually, after watching a couple of reruns of shows I liked, I got up and went to bed to read my book.

The next day was more of the same, I went through all the job search sites, checked my emails to see if any responses had come in, and to reply to any that I could. There were no job offers, but a couple did say they would be setting up interviews for the next week, and I would hear from them with a time and place by the end of the week. Like the day before there were a lot of emails from the adoption search site. I read through them, but none of them really needed my attention.

Wednesday morning I got two phone calls. One from the bookstore for an interview that day if I could make it. Of course I could make it, and I got ready to go. The other call was from the Answering Service. The company was in the same building as a medical equipment company, owned by the same man, and there was a lot of overlap I was told. I made an appointment for the next day to meet for an interview. I felt great heading out of the bookstore interview. He said he had a few other people to interview, but with my history of working at the library with my mom when I was younger, and the fact that I read a lot, I had a good feeling about it.

Thursday I had the interview with the Answering Service. There were two positions available, one in the Answering Service, and one at the front desk, answering the incoming calls for both companies. I preferred the reception desk, only because I had no clue what an answering service was all about. It was a full time position, Monday to Friday, 8 a.m. to 5 p.m. I was hired on the spot. This meant that I would only have Saturdays available to work at the bookstore if they wanted me. I called him when I got home, and explained the situation to him. He was happy for me that I found something full time, and did say that he would like me for Saturdays if I was still available. I said yes, and realized that my job search was over already. I was so lucky to find two jobs in one week, at a time when a lot of people had been looking for months, even years, for a job. Having two jobs also meant I would be free of Tom in no time. Once I started getting my pay cheques I would be able to support myself. Breaking free from Tom completely would be much better for both of us. That way we were both free to move on. I realized he already had moved on, so it was me that needed to. That was happening much quicker than I had expected it to.

Friday I was free to do anything I wanted to do, and I decided it was a good day to do some grocery shopping. I called my girlfriends and invited them over for drinks that evening. They were both able to come, which was great. I would also get a gift basket sent to the rental agent while I was at the store. I picked up a tray of cheese and crackers, and bought fresh vegetables to put out for the girls as well. Shopping and getting the trays ready took me the rest of the morning, so I made some lunch, and sat in the window seat to eat it. After lunch I didn't have any plans, so I went back to the adoption search. There were a couple of emails again from the lady in British Columbia. She said she wanted to help, and when I emailed her back asking her what she was going to charge me she said nothing. She did it for fun, and just genuinely wanted to help people out. I was so touched by that. The fact that a perfect stranger wanted to do that for me was amazing. I didn't think there were many people left in the world like her. Things sure had changed, and I didn't know if it was all for the better. But she made me smile, and that meant a lot to me at the time. Lately I hadn't had much to smile about.

The girls came over that night, and we had some wine, and the party platters I had made up. We had a great night talking, laughing, and just being together. It was so great to be able to do that again, and I was totally relaxed by the time they had to leave. They were both excited about my finding two jobs already, but they worried about me working six days a week. I hadn't really thought about it but I did tell them I was taking the job at the bookstore more for my own pleasure than for the money. I would not tell the owner that though, or my job may turn into a volunteer position.

The weekend was relaxing, other than an email from Tom. Apparently he wanted to move on really quickly, he wanted an address to send the court papers to for my signature. He would file them with the court, and we should have our divorce relatively quickly. That was one thing I had found about the United States when I lived there, they were much quicker to grant divorces, and that was just one thing that had made me realize I was not in Canada over the years I lived there.

I didn't really want him to have my address, or phone number for that matter, so I didn't reply straight away to his email. I decided I would open up a post office box, and that is the address I would give him. If he needed to talk to me over the phone I would tell him I would call him collect. I knew that would make him angry, but, I knew that in time he would probably be living just a couple of hours from me, and I didn't want him showing up at my door. Saturday afternoon I was fortunate to find a place within walking distance where I could open up a post office box. Since I wouldn't need to check it daily it was nice to have it in walking distance, and if I was out for a walk I could just drop in and check it. In the meantime Tom had emailed me back, and this one was more aggressive than the first. He was offended that I wouldn't give him my phone number, but I didn't give in to him. I had made sure that no one could call information and get my number when I set up the phone, so I was pretty confident that he wouldn't be able to easily get my number. I sent him the P.O. Box address, and ignored the fact that he was trying to demand my phone number from me. I had no duty to him anymore, and I was going to make that clear to him. Life was not on his terms anymore when it came to me. He made sure of that when he had started having an affair with my sister-in-law.

Sunday evening I started to feel butterflies in my stomach over starting the new job. I had no doubt that I was more than capable of doing it; it was just the newness of it, and all the new people I would meet. It truly meant that I was well on my way to my new life, and that was very exciting. I had nowhere to go but up from here.

Before I went to bed I got my clothes ready for the next day. I wasn't sure how they wanted me to dress, so I put out pants and a blouse, figuring that would be dressy enough for an office job. I was a very pleased woman that night looking back on my first week alone. I was proud of myself for the things I had accomplished already. I fell asleep with a smile on my face, looking forward to the next stage of my life.

Chapter 16

Monday morning I was up early, had a good breakfast, got dressed, and was able to get to my new job about fifteen minutes early. Since there were only three rows of parking in the lot I parked in the back row and watched the people going in. Most of the women seemed to be around my age, or in their forties. Of course I had no idea who worked where, or did what. I would find out all of that soon enough. About five minutes before I was to be there I headed in. There was a young girl at the reception desk, and she told me she would be training me. She showed me around the building, and explained as we went what the job entailed. I realized while meeting everyone that there were two things going on in my mind. One was I would never remember all their names today, and the other was that I had certainly chosen the right clothes. Most of the people were in jeans, some in dress pants. At least I would not have to put a lot of money out for a new wardrobe, which was great. And I would be comfortable at work. That was a definite plus. Everyone was polite, and most of them wished me well, letting me know that if I had any questions I should feel free to ask. I thought to myself that I liked it here already. The day flew by, but it was a good day. I learned a lot, and at the same time I knew that it wasn't rocket science. Since there were two companies to answer for the phone was clearly labelled for which company the call was coming in for. Tuesday and Wednesday went by just as quickly, and I felt pretty confident that I would be okay on my own, which I didn't know was going to be Thursday. I learned that after lunch on Wednesday, and again I had a few butterflies, but I knew I would be fine on my own, and I also knew that the girls upstairs were there if I had any questions.

Thursday and Friday flew by. The phones were really quite busy there, and any slow times that I had I could basically do what I wanted to do, unless anyone had anything I could do at the desk. I had never been strictly a receptionist, and realized that it could become tedious, but, on the plus side, I got to do anything I wanted while sitting there as long as I had no other work. That meant that I could work on my adoption search at work during the slow times. What a bonus! So after the first week I was starting to feel fairly comfortable in my new position.

Friday night was another girls' night with my friends. We had decided that we would try for every second Friday night, just to get away from everything, have some fun, and do girl things. It goes without saying that we did exactly that. We laughed, we had some serious talks, and just enjoyed being together, making up for all the lost time while I was in the United States.

Saturday I was starting the job at the bookstore, so I was up early again and out the door for the day. It was, again, a pretty simple job. I was receptionist and sales clerk. Since it was a new bookstore it wasn't that busy, so again, I would have time on my hands there as well. Along with the duties of receptionist and sales clerk I had to do some light cleaning. Dusting book shelves and straightening up. There were a few plants to look after. It wasn't a lot of work, but something to keep me busy during the day. Since it was only going to be one day a week, and Saturday at that, I may not have a lot of dusting to do. The girl that worked Monday to Friday would have lots of time to do that. So it was the same as my other new job in the sense that I could fill my slow times with whatever I wanted, as long as I answered the phone and helped the customers. I had no problems with that, and the fact that I could browse the shelves was great. My only fear was that my pay cheque would not cover the books I wanted to buy every week, which turned out to be true some weeks.

When I got home late Saturday afternoon I was glad to know that I didn't have to do it all over the next day. Sundays were probably going to become a very lazy day for me. I would try to get my cleaning and other chores done through the week so that I could just have a "me" day on Sundays. Working two jobs, and only having one day a week off, I really thought I would need Sundays to myself to recharge my batteries and start it all over again on Mondays.

Sunday was just what I expected. It was a lazy day. I hadn't really read any of my emails since Thursday evening, so I decided I would go through those while I was having coffee in the morning. Most of them were from the adoption search sites, so I went through those first and replied to any that I needed to. There was some junk mail; those were easy to get rid of. The last email I had left to read was from Tom. I left it for later. I didn't want to think about him, or anything to do with him. Not right now. I was still on a high from having such a good week, and I just knew that his email would burst that bubble and bring me down. There was one other email that had come in while I was reading all the others. It was from the woman in British Columbia. It was a short one, asking me if I used any of the messengers on the internet. I didn't, but she said that she used MSN, so I decided to download it and start an account. I emailed her back with my username, and she must have been at her computer when I sent it because I had a request from her right away, and that now meant we could chat there, instead of doing it all in email. That seemed like a great idea, and we then proceeded to chat for the next couple of hours. I told her about my jobs, and how the week had gone, and I could just tell by her responses that she was going to be a mother figure to me. She would keep me grounded, give me advice, but also she was such a joyful and positive person that I was sure I would be nothing but happy around her. I was not good at letting people into my life, and this latest episode with Tom had reinforced my thoughts that letting people in would get me hurt. Talking over the internet was fine for me, but I wasn't prepared yet to put too much out there. With time our chats would become much more personal, and I would gradually let her into my heart.

Later that day, as I reflected on the week that had just passed, and the week that was to come, I was content. But most of all I was proud of myself for being able to move forward and not falling into a pit of sorrow over the past. I knew that the past happened for a reason, and that the times to come would only help me move forward. My last thought of the day was my adoption search, and how, right now, it was sort of at a standstill. But hopefully I would get my non-identifying information soon, and then begin a full on search for my birth family.

Chapter 17

Monday evening I decided it was time to deal with Tom's email. I opened it up and started to read. Just reading it made me angry. He was demanding to know why I hadn't sent the paperwork in yet for the divorce. To be quite honest, I had forgotten about the divorce papers, and hadn't checked the post office box for over a week. I was not going to jump up and run out to check it either. It could wait until tomorrow night, if I remembered to stop on my way home from work. I sent an email back to him telling him that he had no right to demand anything of me anymore. He chose to have an affair, and, essentially, he ended our marriage. He didn't care about me, my hopes, and my dreams. He put himself first, as I realized now that he always did, and he didn't care about the path of destruction he left in his wake. When I finally sent the email I realized that I had been holding those thoughts in, and it felt good to get it all off my chest. I was not looking forward to his next email, but I was very thankful that he didn't have my phone number. As far as I was concerned he would never have it. There was no need for him to have it.

Releasing those feelings left me feeling exhausted, and I decided to call it a night, even though it was early yet, and took my book to bed.

I woke in the middle of the night from a dream I was having. It wasn't a scary dream, but there was a lot of tension. By the time I was alert enough to realize that it was a dream I couldn't remember it. I got up to get some water, and went back to bed. I was still thinking about the dream, trying to remember, but I just couldn't recall any of it. Looking back, I think my life would have taken a different turn if I could have remembered that dream.

Chapter 18

My life the next couple of weeks was pretty uneventful. I sent the papers Tom wanted, and had a couple of not so nice emails from him, but other than that nothing much happened. That was fine with me; I needed normal for a while. I was settling into the job as a receptionist, and as much as I liked the job at the bookstore I was finding that I was more tired each week. It might not have been such a good idea to take two jobs. One day off a week just wasn't enough it seemed. I had to make a decision about the bookstore. I was still thinking about it when I met up with the girls on a Friday night at a local pub. We were having dinner that night; usually it was just a couple of hours in the evening that we took to get together. Having a little more time with them was great. I needed the distraction that night. I talked to them about both jobs, and told them I was considering letting the one at the bookstore go, as much as I hated to. If the bookstore had been able to offer me full time hours it would have been my dream job, unfortunately that wasn't meant to be. I also told them about the goings on with Tom, and they were of the same mind as me, he had no right to demand anything from me, or to write the emails that he had written. The girls filled me in on what was going on with them, and then we just let our hair down and had fun. There was karaoke at the pub, and we had a lot of fun listening to people that thought they could sing.

At one point during the night the waitress brought me a beer that I hadn't ordered and told me it was from the guy at the bar. We all had a good laugh. I thought that only happened in the movies. Eventually he came over to the table to introduce himself. His name was James, and we invited him to join us. He was very personable, and was very attentive to everything I said. I'll admit it was nice to see that look on a man's face again, and know that it was me he was giving that look to. After he had been with us for an hour or so he said he needed to get going. He was on call that weekend, he was in medical school. Wow, a doctor interested in me? That was thrilling. He asked for my phone number, and said that he would call soon.

James called me Saturday evening and said he wanted to give me a quick call to thank me for the fun last night. He couldn't talk long, he was still at the hospital, but had a couple of minutes to call me. I was flattered but at the same time there was something inside me that was making me uneasy. If only I had listened to that little voice. But I didn't.

Sunday afternoon James called again, and asked me when we could see each other again. I told him that my week was all work, and I really would not be good company in the evening during the week. If I had been honest with myself, the bells were going off in my head, but I was ignoring them. Or, if I wasn't ignoring them I was trying to convince myself that they were going off because of what had happened with Tom. We ended the call by deciding to meet the following Sunday at the pub again.

By the time the next Sunday rolled around I had serious doubts about seeing James, but I had no way to contact him, so I decided I would go. If I felt uncomfortable I would leave shortly after I got there. When I arrived he was there already, so I sat down at the table and ordered a drink. Again he was so attentive to me, and wanted to know all about me. I did notice that when I asked him about his life he was very vague. That seemed strange to me, but I let it go. Some people don't like talking about their lives, and maybe he was one of them. The afternoon passed quickly, and I left shortly after we had something to eat. The big thing I noticed was that he didn't even offer to pay for my dinner, and certainly not my drinks. But, again, I told myself that's because he's in medical school, and probably didn't have a lot of extra money. I let that go too. Overall we had had a good time. But I still had those alarm bells ringing in my head.

During the week I talked to my girlfriends about James. They both wondered if it was too soon after what had happened with Tom and that was why I was feeling the way I was. That made sense. Since Tom had told me about his affair my life had been a whirlwind. And now when it was just starting to settle down a little I meet this man, so I convinced myself that it was all in my mind.

I didn't hear from him for almost another three weeks, and by that time I had decided that he wasn't calling again, and that was really okay with me. I was still broken, and I needed time to heal, and to figure out who I was, and what I wanted, before I got involved with another man.

One Friday night I happened to drive by where I had rented the post office box, and since I wasn't in a rush to get anywhere I decided I would stop in and check to see if there was anything there. There was, and it was quite a thick letter. From Tom's lawyer. When I got home I threw it on my desk, and forgot about it until Sunday when I sat down there to have a coffee in the morning. The day before had been my last day at the bookstore. I had decided that it was just too much. I was tired all the time, and thought maybe having one more day off a week would be the cure. I was sad to let the job go because I did really enjoy it, but they couldn't give me full time hours, and I couldn't afford to only work one day a week. I had also gone that week and got myself a library card. With the library having a website online, I could reserve books on there and pick them up when they were available. If I didn't have anything specific in mind that I wanted to read then I would go in and wander around the library until I found something. I would be saving a lot of money as well by not working at the bookstore because I wouldn't be so tempted to buy every new book. So Sunday morning when I sat at my desk I was not thinking about Tom at all, I was thinking about how I would miss the job, and the one friend that I had made there. I knew that Carolyn and I would remain friends, but I wouldn't see her as much now. She was only there part time too, but we usually worked together every Saturday morning. She was a lot of fun, and just a couple of years younger than me. We would definitely keep in contact.

I sat there looking at the letter and decided I should open it. I had no idea how long it had been in the mailbox, and I had a feeling that I would probably be getting another nasty email from Tom soon if I didn't open it and deal with whatever was in it. I was quite shocked to see an inventory list when I opened it up, and even more shocked to see that many things that I had brought with me Tom figured I should take back to him. I just laughed. I couldn't believe how brazen he was. He was the one that ruined the marriage, that killed my dream of having children, and he wanted me to give in to his demands now? There was no way I was giving anything back to him, and since I never wanted him to know where I was living he was never going to come and get anything. I typed up a letter, stating that I would not sign the inventory list, and if he wanted to fight me on it then I would just stop the proceedings all together. After all, he was the one involved with another woman, and I was sure that it would be a long time before I ever really needed the divorce. I sure did not plan on being married again. In fact, right now, I couldn't even see myself in a relationship. I printed off a copy of the letter stating just that, and put it in an envelope addressed to his lawyer. I also copied the letter into an email for Tom, and waited for the firestorm I was surely about to cause.

The rest of that Sunday I spent working around my apartment, and in the early evening James called. He wanted to meet with me that night, and when I said no, that I had to work in the morning he seemed rather upset. Could we get together Monday evening, he asked. I decided that I would go, and made sure to tell him it was for dinner only, I had work in the morning again. He agreed, but I could tell he wanted more. I put it out of my mind, did a few things around the apartment, and went to bed not giving it another thought.

Chapter 19

Dinner on Monday evening was fun, and James paid this time for everything. He wanted to come back to my place, but I was not ready for him, or any man for that matter, to be in my apartment. My apartment was my sanctuary, and I did not want it invaded. Not until I was more comfortable with where this relationship was going. He seemed a little offended, but I told him again that I wasn't ready for any man to be there, it wasn't just him. We were really just barely getting to know one another, and I knew I was not ready for any kind of commitment with anyone as of yet. Maybe I was being too cautious, but my heart and soul were still mending, and until I knew that the healing was done, I would not be able to give myself to another relationship, not completely, and I felt that any less would not be fair to the man I was with.

When we parted that night he asked me if I could at least give him a ride downtown. I hadn't realized until then that he didn't have a car. Of course I can, I said. So we got in my car and I dropped him in front of a building close to the hospital. He invited me up, but I declined. If I wasn't ready to have him in my home, I certainly wasn't ready to be in his home. Driving away I saw him watching me in the rear view mirror. When I got further down the street I was sure that I saw him walking away from the building towards downtown, which I found rather odd. By the time I got home I had forgotten about it, and had decided he probably wouldn't call me again. I still had no way to get in touch with him. He said he didn't have a home phone right then, and no computer. So if we were to talk, it would be when he felt like calling. That was okay with me, and I should have known by the way I felt then that I should have never seen him again. But I did. Eventually it was to become one of the biggest regrets of my life.

Chapter 20

The next few weeks were quiet for me. I was feeling settled in my new life, and was ready to move on to the next chapter. I hoped that that chapter was going to be happier than the last one had been. I did a lot of reflecting during this time, and tried to chalk the past up to life experience. I also tried to see the good in all that had happened. That was the difficult part. I guess I wasn't quite ready to put all the hurt behind me yet, and I was still not quite comfortable trusting my own decisions at that point. I wanted to believe that I would never let myself be had like that again, but looking back over my life I had always been a trusting person, and took people and life at face value. I certainly did not want to become a cynic, and I had to find the happy medium. I had to find a way to protect myself from that kind of pain again.

During this time I did a lot of thinking about my adoption search. I was ready to move forward with it, and sometime mid-February my non-identifying information came in the mail. I read it over and over and over the first week that I had it. I think I had it memorized, which was probably a good thing because the pages were looking worn already, curling from turning them over, and from tears as well. I found out a lot of things that I never knew. My birth mother had had me with her for eleven days; she didn't give me up in the hospital as I was told by my adoptive mother. I found out that I had a half-brother as well. He was two years older than me, and that was the first time I had ever given any thought to having an older sibling. I don't know why, but I always thought I would have younger siblings, and that I would have been her first child. So now not only did I want to find my birth mother, but I had a brother I wanted to find as well. I didn't know if he knew about me, but chances are he didn't. My birth mother had left her home province of Newfoundland and moved to Toronto before she was pregnant with me, and she had left my brother at home with his grandparents, my grandparents. There was a lot more information contained in those pages, and I was hopeful that maybe it would get me a few steps closer to finding my family.

I was still seeing James occasionally during this time, and I don't know if the bells had stopped ringing, or if I was just ignoring them. He had told me a little more about himself and his life during this time, and I found out that he was adopted as well. He was born to a woman from Prince Edward Island, but adopted by a couple in the United States, where he had grown up and lived until he found his birth mother about five years earlier. His adoptive parents were both dead, and he was an only child, so when he found his birth mother he decided to stay in Canada, to try to foster a relationship with her. Unfortunately, after a couple of years, the relationship just didn't take off. She would be in contact with him regularly, then drop off the map, then come back after a few months, and he just didn't want the drama that had been involved. I could understand that, or so I thought. I was still living in my little bubble, thinking that there could not possibly be any reason why a birth mother would not welcome her child with open arms. I was finding out that that wasn't always the case.

James certainly wanted a serious relationship much faster than I did. It had only been a few months since my marriage had ended, and to say I was a little gun shy was an understatement. I was terrified to let anyone into my heart again, and I know that was frustrating for James. I tried to explain it to him, but I just couldn't seem to get through to him. All my life I had been able to walk away from the things that had caused me the most pain, sometimes with regrets, but I was always able to bounce back quickly. This time it just wasn't happening. I thought maybe it was because I had been so close to realizing my dream of becoming a mother, and there was more than just my heart that had been crushed this time.

I did finally invite him over for dinner one Sunday evening in February, not Valentine's Day because I didn't want him to get any more ideas than he already had about where we were, or where we were headed, in the relationship. It was closer to the end of the month when I finally let him into my sanctuary.

The dinner went well, he was still very attentive to me, but I felt him pushing a little harder every time we were together. I decided there was no time like the present to address the problem once again. I tried to explain to him that I was having fun seeing him once in a while, but that I just wasn't ready to get serious so quickly. I had done a lot of soul searching in the past few months, but I knew there was still a lot of work for me to do on myself before I could let someone in. I thought he was at least trying to understand, but he did say that he wasn't going to stop, until I either fell in love with him, or just gave in to his pressure. He had said it in what I thought was a joking tone of voice, but, honestly, if I had really listened I would have heard the not so friendly undertone. In fact, since it was getting pretty late on Sunday night, and the buses had stopped running, he said he didn't have enough for cab fare, and I had had some wine and didn't want to risk driving, so he ended up spending the night on my couch. Monday morning I dropped him off at the hospital on my way to work, but when I got home after work he was waiting for me. I should have stopped it then, but I didn't, and James basically moved in that day. Until that final night, many months later, when it all came crashing down, and my life was in ruins once again.

Looking back, I know now that if I ever hear those bells ringing in my head again, or even the hint of them, I will listen, and run like the Devil is chasing me. If he taught me nothing else, it was to follow my instincts, something that I, up until then, thought I had been reasonably good at doing. I certainly wasn't that time, and because of that, I almost lost my life.

I knew within weeks, if not days, that James was not the same man I had met that first night at the bar. In the months to come I would unravel his life, bit by bit, and what I uncovered was nothing like I had been told in the beginning.

The first week was hard for me, having someone in my sanctuary, and having to adjust my life around him. We did have some great talks, and generally got along quite well. It was an adjustment period for both of us, and anything that occurred that first couple of weeks I tried to chalk up to that fact. The first thing I noticed was that he had very little in the way of possessions. Very few clothes and he didn't want to move any furniture in at all. When I asked him about it he said that he still had his apartment, where I had dropped him off more than once, and would have until the end of April to get everything out and moved over to my place. That raised a lot of questions. I wasn't willing to part with any of my things; I had just started out recently, and was proud of my place and my things. First he questioned me about that, wanting to know why I didn't want his belongings there. For one thing, I had never stepped foot in his apartment, nor had I seen any of his things. I liked the way my place looked, and I didn't want a bunch of furniture that didn't fit in. He finally said that was fine, he would rent a storage unit until the time came when we either moved, or wanted to make the place ours instead of mine. The second thing I noticed was that for someone that was in medical school, he had no books, and I never saw him doing any type of homework. Suddenly he was home every night and weekend as well. He told me that he was done his term at the hospital, and was back in classes. Being that I worked every night until at least 5 pm he was able to get his work done before I got home, either at the library or at home. He sounded convincing, and I let him convince me. The third thing I couldn't help but notice was that he had a severe lack of funds. He never offered to pay for anything, whether it was groceries, utilities, rent, entertainment, nothing. When I would broach the subject he said he was living on student loans, and just had no extra money. But once he was a doctor he would be able to take care of me as well as the bills. That sounded good to me at the time. The question was how did I make enough money to support him and myself for the next few years? He said he would start looking for a part time job, which I thought was strange. I didn't know any other medical students, but I was pretty sure they probably didn't have "after school" jobs with their workload. Eventually we fell into a pattern of work and school, and finding common interests during our off time.

Before the end of April I started to see signs of James' possessiveness. He wanted all of my time, and didn't want me to have contact with my friends. I was frustrated about that, and in order to keep the peace I started getting together with my friends over lunches when we could. I missed the girls' nights out, as did they, and I could tell they were frustrated by my willingness to let him control me the way I was. We started to see each other less and less as the months went on, until eventually almost all contact was broken off.

In June James hit me for the first time. He was so upset that he had done it, and was so apologetic I let it go, but told him that if he ever did it again he was out. It should have been the first and the last time that he hit me. It wasn't.

One day when I met my girlfriends for lunch I was sure that I saw James across the street from the coffee shop. I wasn't positive, but I had a funny feeling that it was him. I didn't like that feeling. If he was in the area, and had seen me, why wouldn't he come and talk to me. Maybe I hadn't seen him, just someone that resembled him. By the time I got home from work that night I had forgotten about it. But then I started to see him hanging around the building I worked in. I was sure it was him, but when I would ask him if he was in the area he would deny it, saying he didn't have time to follow me with all the work that he had to do. But I couldn't get past that feeling that I had; that feeling like I was being watched, or followed. Over time we fought about it more than once, because he could never tell me where he had been at the times I thought I saw him, and told me it was really none of my business anyway. I couldn't believe he said that, since he demanded to know everything I did, and everyone I saw or talked to, every bloody day. I told him it wasn't fair, and that was the second time he hit me. I told him I was going to call the police, and that he needed to get out now if he didn't want me to call them. He left that night. He came to my office the next day with flowers, and was extremely apologetic. He wanted to come home, and I said that I didn't think that was a good idea. He made me feel so guilty because he had nowhere to go, and no money for a room, so I let him come home. Biggest mistake ever. From there on things between us were rocky, and headed downhill quickly.

We started fighting about everything, from the way he put dirty dishes in the sink, to the fact that he never helped me around the house with any of the chores, and the most contentious point was the fact that I still had to pay for everything. I didn't make a lot of money. I was able to live comfortably on my own, and still had a little left over to have fun with. But I wasn't able to support us both, and I found it getting more and more difficult every week. He was always asking me for money. Not asking, demanding. At first it was small amounts, walking around money. Then the amounts went up and up and up, until I started saying no. The arguments got worse and worse. One night he stormed out of the apartment, saying that if he stayed he was going to seriously hurt me. So he left. I slammed the door after him, and started to cry. I didn't understand how I had let this happen. I wasn't stupid. I knew there was something very wrong with this situation right from the start, but I had let him sweet talk me, and by that time he had almost absolute control over me and everything I did. I started to get angry, and realized that I had to do something about this. I couldn't let this continue, and deep down, I knew he had not been kidding about seriously hurting me.

I realized he had left without taking his back pack with him. In all the time he had been here he had never left home without it. I had asked him on a couple of occasions what he had in there that was so important because if I ever went near it he became very agitated and told me it was his, the only thing that was his alone in the whole place, and it was going to stay that way. I had no right to look in the bag, or question him about the contents. I grabbed a beer from the fridge, and sat on the couch staring at that damn back pack. I felt like if I opened it, he would walk through the door just as I did. But, I hadn't put the chain lock on the door when I had slammed it. If I did and he came home I would have to let him in. I put the chain on the door, and sat on the couch with the bag.

I was about to feel like I was living in a movie. Things like this just didn't happen. Not to me at least. But they could, and did.

Chapter 21

When I opened James' back pack I found it was full of papers, and a lot of junk. At least it would have been junk to me. Key chains, kids toys from fast food restaurants, but I guess they all had some kind of meaning to him. What I didn't find was anything that would indicate he was a medical student, or anything to indicate he was a student of any kind. I was puzzled, and knew that I had to get to the bottom of all of this. So I started leafing through the papers as quickly as I could, in case he came back and caught me. I knew that would just be another huge fight if he did.

Most of the papers were meaningless to me. But what I did come across that had any relevance to me blew me away. I was stunned, and just sat there not knowing what to do. First I found identification papers, and a photo id, with a completely different name on them. Certainly not the name that I knew him by, and with the photo identification in front of me, there was no question that it was James. Or should I say Luke. Luke Clare. I also found papers with the name I knew him by, James Peterson.

What was I supposed to do with this information? And why did he have two identities?

I have to admit that I was more than just a little scared by then. I didn't know who he really was, James or Luke. And whichever one he was, was that the name I knew him by? The only thing I could think was why? And what was he running from? Or who was he running from?

What had I gotten myself involved in? I was sitting on the couch, in complete disbelief, and hoping this was just a bad dream. But it wasn't. I had no clue what to do, so I kept digging.

Deeper into the pile I found welfare pay stubs. What? He was on welfare? I checked the dates, and sure enough, as long as I had known him he had been on welfare. I knew the name of the street I had dropped him off on a few times, in front of the building where he supposedly had a place, and the address on them was not that building.

I decided I had to write down everything I had found, and put everything back in the back pack. Since he hadn't come back, or phoned, I decided to get on the internet, and find out where the address was that was on the welfare stubs. It turned out to be a men's homeless shelter. Again, I was dumbfounded. Again my life was falling apart, and it was all lies. From the moment I met him it had all been lies. I felt all the pain and anger welling up inside of me, and I started to cry again. I didn't know if I could make it through another heart break. I cried until there were no more tears. When I finally came out of my stupor I realized it was dark, and he hadn't come back yet. I knew he would show up eventually, and I was on edge. Truthfully I didn't want him to come back. As far as I was concerned it was over. Whatever it was that we had was done. I wanted nothing to do with him. The trust was gone. I would never again believe anything that came out of his mouth.

I didn't know what to do, and figured there was nothing I could do that night, so I tried to get myself ready for the week to come, and eventually fell into bed, completely exhausted, and cried myself to sleep.

Chapter 22

Monday morning I woke up feeling like I was in a fog. James had not come home. I had not slept much, and I was so confused and tired. I went through the motions of getting ready for work, and left my home, which no longer felt like my sanctuary anymore. It was like a nightmare. All the feelings I had just gotten past about Tom were now back, and this time they were worse. Not only was I sad, and angry at James, but I was really upset with myself as well for letting this happen to me again.

This was the first time since starting this job that I didn't want to be there. I didn't want to be at home both because I was sure that when I got there James would be there too, and if I had been able to admit it to myself, I was scared to be in the apartment alone with him. I made it through the morning, but by lunch time I was so physically and mentally exhausted that I decided I had to talk to my boss to see if I could leave work for the day.

I called Elliot, my boss, in his office and asked him if I could speak with him. He said sure, and I headed upstairs to his office. Elliot was only a few years older than me, and during my time there he and his wife had become friends of mine, not just in the context of work, but outside of work as well. They were great people, and we had a lot of the same interests. I knew from the start that Elliot didn't care for James, but he respected my space and never voiced his opinions. As soon as I walked into his office he knew something had happened over the weekend. I could see the concern in his face and hear it in his voice, and that was all it took to start my tears. It felt like I cried for hours before I was able to talk, but it was only a couple of minutes. In that space of a couple of minutes the worry on Elliot's face became worse and worse. He took my hands gently and pulled me into a hug. It was just what I needed, and that hug made me realize I wasn't alone in this. I had people I could depend on for support, and that gave me the strength to start telling him what was going on.

When I was done telling him what I had found out the day before, he was in shock. He was angry as well. By telling him all of it the door was open for him to tell me how he really felt about James. It was worse than I had imagined. He really didn't like him before, and now this made him livid.

Once he calmed down, he asked me what I was going to do. I had no clue, and told him that what I really wanted right now was just to go home, have a beer and a long hot bath, and hopefully sleep until the next day. He agreed that I should do just that, but I could tell he was worried about what would happen when I did get home if James was there. Or when James did come back. He was genuinely in fear for my safety, but I told him I thought I would be okay. For that day at least because I had no clue what I was going to do with the information I had gathered, and I was certainly not going to let on that I had found any of it. Elliot asked me if he could keep the notes I had made, partly because he didn't want James to happen to come across them, but also because he wanted to delve deeper into the mystery of this man. I agreed that it was better that way, and I knew that what I had told him would go no further than his office. He did ask me if he could tell his wife, and I told him to go ahead, it would be one less person I would have to tell. He followed me home, just to make sure that I was going to be okay in case James was there. It turned out that he wasn't, but his back pack was gone, so he had been there. I found a note from him, a nasty one that said we were going to talk, with the word talk in quotes. Elliot didn't want me staying there, and I told him that it was my home, and I couldn't let him drive me out of it. I assured him that he would be my second phone call if things got out of hand when James came home, my first call would be to the police. He then handed me his cell phone, and told me to hide it in a pocket or in my car, so that if James tried to keep me from making any calls I could use his phone.

On his way out he put the phone in the glove box in my car, and made sure it was locked up. I put the chain on the door and went to the fridge to get a beer. I sat on my window seat and just stared out the window, slowly drinking my beer, and feeling the exhaustion taking over. I was so tired in fact, that I skipped the bath, and just went right to bed. I didn't wake up until after dark. Hearing James's keys in the door was what woke me, and I jumped out of bed suddenly feeling very anxious. Luckily I had unintentionally left the door chain off when I had come home.

I had to compose myself, and pretend that I didn't know what I knew, but most of all, I couldn't let him figure it out. I took a few deep breaths, and walked out to the living room. He was sitting on the couch, and before I could say anything he got up and came towards me, apologizing, and wanting to hug me. I backed away from him, not wanting him to touch me. I just told him we needed to talk, and that I wasn't ready to kiss and make up yet. I could tell that made him angry, but he didn't say or do anything. He just stood there, in the middle of the living room, asking me what he could do to make it better.

I wanted so badly to tell him what I knew. I wanted to scream at him that I knew he was a fraud, and a liar. But I held it in, and told him that I didn't know what he could do, but things had to change or he would have to leave for good. I saw tears in his eyes, but still felt nothing, other than some warped sense of awe that he could cry on command apparently. I went to the kitchen to find something to eat, and he just sat back down and turned the television on. As far as I could tell he thought everything was going to be fine. He acted like it was a normal Monday night, football and all. I found a frozen dinner to eat, and went back to bed. I heard him come to bed later, but pretended I was asleep. I didn't want to start any kind of conversation with him until I had my bearings again, and had a plan.

Chapter 23

Tuesday morning I got up and got ready for work. James was still asleep, so I was sure to be quiet and not wake him. That was both for him and for me. I didn't want to get into anything with him before I left, so if he was sleeping it was a perfect way to avoid it. When I got to work Elliot called me into his office. He had another girl watch my desk for me, so I knew it wasn't going to be a short conversation.

He closed his door, and asked me how I was doing. I told him I was okay, considering. He just nodded. I told him that James had come home, and wanted to kiss and make up, but I didn't let him off the hook, and he was still sleeping when I left that morning. I could see the relief on his face. Then he said that he had done a lot of thinking, and talking with his wife, the night before. There were a few things that he wanted to talk to me about. Things that he thought would make things a little easier for me.

The first thing was that he wanted to know if I would be willing to learn the answering service side of the business, and explained why. After talking at length with his wife the previous evening, they thought that maybe I could be safer if I varied my routine. Since the answering service was a 24 hours a day, 7 days a week operation, the operators worked shift work. Everyone worked every shift, so if I did start to work there I would be on shift work as well. I asked him to give me some time to think about it.

He continued on saying that they had done a little researching last night. They Googled James with both names, and came up with very little information. They did, however, find that James's parents were alive and well and living in New Jersey. He wasn't an only child either. He had an older sister, and younger brother. Both alive and well, and living in New Jersey. Of course, this was all based on the name Luke Clare. The name James

Peterson garnered very little information, leading Elliot to believe that James Peterson was not his real name. The question remained though, why did he fake his existence, and everything about his life as James Peterson?

I asked him if they had found any information in regards to medical school, knowing deep down what the answer was going to be. No. There was no indication in anything they found that said he was a medical student. I wasn't surprised at all by then. The only emotion I was feeling was dread at that point.

Elliot wanted me to take the day off, to think about the answering service position, and a few other things he had yet to tell me. I was worried that James would be there, and wondered out loud if he ever left or went anywhere, other than to run out before I got home and come back in acting like he had been gone all day. I felt so foolish, so betrayed, and so mad that I had let another man completely turn my world inside out again. Tonya, Elliot's wife, was a stay at home mom, and with both of their boys being in school full time now she was available during the day for almost anything that came up. She had passed a message through Elliot that their spare bedroom had clean sheets, the meaning being obvious. But again, I didn't want to let James drive me out of my own home.

I did decide to at least meet Tonya for coffee, just to have a distraction for a while before I had to face James again.

Elliot wasn't done talking yet. He had a few other things he wanted me to think about.

Did I want him to get in touch with James's family to see if he could get me any information that might let us all know why he had created a new life?

Did I want them to contact the police to see what my options were regarding getting James out of my apartment? That was an easy one for me to answer. Since they weren't directly involved I knew that the police weren't really going to be able to give them anything other than general information. But, I did know that he had not let the welfare office know he was living with me. He still had the men's shelter address on his monthly cheque stubs. If they knew it would have affected his monthly cheque I'm sure, and more than likely he would get much less money, or possibly none at all. Not that that mattered to me, since he had never contributed a dime to anything. It made me wonder what he did with the money every month, and what did he do every day when he said he was at school? Did he just sit at home? Did he go out, and if he did, where?

My thinking aloud had led to Elliot's next question. Did I want them to call the welfare office and report him? No, not yet. Did I want them to call and find out what the options were? That was okay with me. Any information I could get would be helpful. So he said he would make the call as soon as I left. I knew that Elliot would still keep trying to come up with information, as much as he could, but that he would never act on any of it without talking to me about it first.

Before I left the office I handed Elliot his cell phone. He thought I should keep it, but I said I couldn't. I couldn't inconvenience him that way; I knew he spent a lot of the day on that phone, dealing with work. He took it back, under protest of course. I gathered up my purse and coat, and headed out to meet Tonya for coffee, and possibly lunch, with the promise that I would seriously consider the position at the answering service.

Chapter 24

On my way to meet Tonya I tried to process the new information I had, and come up with some good reason why James had lied about everything about his life. I just couldn't come up with any reasonable explanation. He was running from something, but what?

I shouldn't have been worrying about that I realized. I should be figuring out how to get him out of my life without being seriously injured doing it. I hadn't told Elliot, or anyone for that matter, about James hitting me. I was so ashamed that I had let him, and let him stay after it had happened. Eventually I would tell people, but not until James was out of my life for good, and I knew that no more harm would come to me by telling them.

I got to the restaurant before Tonya, so I got a coffee and a booth by the window. I was in such a daze when she walked up to the table that she startled me. She didn't say anything at first, just looked at me with such sorrow, and my tears threatened to start again. I didn't want to cry anymore, so I jumped up and hugged her, telling her I was okay, and would remain okay, no matter where this path took me. She sat down, and we talked about her boys, and anything else we could come up that didn't involve James. Finally we had exhausted everything, and were left with the elephant sitting on the table between us.

Tonya said that she was so sorry for all of this, and that she and Elliot were there for anything I needed, day or night. It was good to know I had them in my corner, and I told her as much. I reassured her that I was fine right now, and that I had to come up with a plan. Without the research they had done, I wouldn't be able to come up with anything, and I would definitely keep them in the loop at every step of the way.

Tonya then handed me a small gift bag with a bow on it. I asked her what it was, and she told me to open it. It was a cell phone, already activated, with a card with the number on it. I told her I couldn't take it, and she said I could, and I would. It was on their plan, unlimited everything, and that I needed to keep it with me at all times. She had programmed her cell number, Elliot's cell number, and their home number into it, and told me I was expected to use those numbers anytime I needed to.

I was humbled by their gift, and said I couldn't thank them enough. My only worry was what I was going to tell James should he discover I had a cell phone. Easy, she said, and she proceeded to call Elliot. She asked Elliot if he could make me assistant manager of something at work. Anything would do. But whatever it was, I had to be on call 24/7. Hence the need for the cell phone. It was a great plan, and Elliot instantly made me the assistant manager of client accounts. It was the strangest title I had ever heard, and I thought that James would question it as well. So then he made me Shift Manager of the answering service.

In that instant he had made my decision for me about training for the answering service. I couldn't tell James that I had the position if I wasn't working for that part of the company. And since that decision was made, I would start training the following week.

Tonya and I had lunch, and I decided it was time to face the music and go home. I told her I would call if anything happened, and we both got in our cars and drove away. On the way home I thought about the answering service, and the shift work, and realized that Elliot was right. Having a schedule that varied was probably a good idea, and switching up the routine at home might be enough to throw James off his game. That was my hope, along with the hope that when I got home I would be alone in the apartment. That wasn't to be. He was there, and it wasn't going to be a very good afternoon.

Chapter 25

I walked in the door that Tuesday afternoon, and my apartment had been torn apart. Papers that had been on my desk were all over the floor, drawers were opened, and some emptied. If James had not been sitting on the couch, waiting for me, I would have thought there had been a burglary at my place. James just sat there quietly staring at me, and it sent a shiver down my spine. He had an evil look on his face, and I knew the fireworks were about to begin. I took a deep breath, took off my coat and hung it up, and walked into the kitchen to get some water. He followed me into the kitchen, still just staring at me, not saying a word. I stared back for a moment, and walked into the bedroom to change my clothes. Again, there he was, silently following me. He had been through every drawer in the bedroom as well. The place was a complete mess, and I was fighting the urge to scream at him, while the tears threatened to start flowing. I kept my back to him, and started to pick things up. He walked over to me, ripped the clothes out of my hands, and slapped me across the face hard enough to knock me off my balance. I fell back towards the bed, and he came at me, fists flying. I screamed at him to stop, and somehow I found the strength to get him off of me, and I was able to get out of the room. I ran for the doorway, hoping to grab my coat and purse, and get to my car before he could catch me. I didn't make it any farther than the doorway.

The scariest part of all of this was that he had still not said one word. I was terrified at that moment.

After he caught me at the door and dragged me back to the living room by my hair he punched me in the face and head, all over my body, until he was tired out. I was crying and scared for my life, almost wishing he would kill me. At least then I would know it was the last time he would beat me. When he finally stopped I laid there on the floor crying, curled up in the fetal position. I had no idea how much time had passed, but I didn't think it had been very long. At the same time it had felt like hours. I heard him in the kitchen, and I tried to get up. As soon as I raised my head I was dizzy, and I tried to at least crawl to the couch. I guess he saw me, or heard me, and he ran into the room again, stomped on my back so hard that it knocked the wind out of me for a second, and forced me to the floor again. I couldn't believe this. I just curled up again, with my hands over my head, trying to protect myself in case he wasn't done yet. I guess he figured that he had done enough, and I heard him walk to the couch.

"Get up bitch," he said.

I tried to stand up, but I was still dizzy, and all I could manage to do was lean myself against the coffee table, not quite sitting up, but not laying on the floor either. I had blood on my hands, and I had no idea where it was coming from. The pain was so intense I felt nauseous, and dizzy. I was afraid I was going to pass out, so I tried to take some deep breaths, hoping that would help. The wave of nausea passed, and I laid my head on the coffee table.

"I said, get up, bitch." The tone of his voice terrified me. There was no emotion in it at all. How could he be so calm when I was so terrified?

I tried to get up again, and through my tears said that I couldn't. I was so scared he was going to beat me more because I wasn't doing what he wanted. I heard him get up and walk towards me, and my whole body tensed up, and I was shaking with fear. He grabbed my arm, pulled me up and threw me towards the bathroom.

"Get in there and clean yourself up. You're disgusting." Still in that cold, emotionless tone.

It hurt to move, but slowly I managed to get my clothes off, and stood under the shower crying. My legs weren't going to hold me up any longer, so I sat in the tub, letting the hot water run over me, watching all the blood run down the drain. I hoped I was in a very bad dream, but I knew better.

Eventually, once the hot water started to run out, I turned off the taps, and literally crawled over the edge of the tub to get a towel and dry off. Leaning on the tub, and using all the strength I had left, I managed to stand up, and get my robe on. I could see the bruises starting to show up all over, and I knew that I was going to be even sorer in the morning.

I took a deep breath, a shaky one, and walked slowly out of the bathroom towards the bedroom.

I didn't even look to see where James was. I didn't care. All I wanted was to crawl under the covers and wish this day away. And then I heard him walk into the bedroom. Just when I thought he couldn't possibly hurt me anymore, he forced himself on me. I screamed and tried to push him off me, but I just had no fight left in me. He covered my mouth and told me to shut up. This was entirely my own fault according to him.

It seemed to last forever, and I tried to turn my mind off, and somehow fool myself into believing it wasn't happening. I couldn't do it. He was raping me. I remember every detail to this day. I think I will remember it until the day I die. Not that I want to, but, something like that just doesn't go away.

I finally fell asleep at some point, and woke up in the middle of the night to find him in bed beside me. For one blissful moment I forgot about it all. Until I tried to move. Every inch of my body was in pain. I was so repulsed by the sight of him sleeping beside me I couldn't get out of bed fast enough. When I did manage to sit up, and finally stand up, I went to the kitchen and made a hot cup of tea. I sat in the window seat, and cried some more.

I don't know how long I sat there, but I woke up with my head against the window, still holding my mug. I had finished the tea at least, so I must have been awake for a while. It didn't matter anyway. Daylight was coming, and somehow I had to make myself presentable, and get to work.

When I finally saw my face in the mirror I was horrified. My eyes were both blackened, with a rather large cut above the left one. I didn't know how I was going to cover this up, and even though the last place I wanted to be was in the same place as him, I knew there was no way I could go to work that day. I waited until 7 am to call Elliot at home and tell him I wouldn't be in that day, and possibly not the rest of the week. I could hear the concern in his voice, and I knew he could tell by my voice that nothing was okay, but somehow he understood that I couldn't say more right then. I didn't know if James was awake and listening to me or not, and I couldn't risk saying anything that would set him off again. I'm sure that Elliot knew without me saying what had happened. I was betting that Elliot knew it wasn't the first time either.

I hung up the phone and lay on the couch, hoping to get some more sleep.

Chapter 26

When I woke up it was almost noon. I had no idea if James was still there or not. I lay there listening to see if I could hear him. I didn't hear anyone moving around, but that didn't mean he was gone. He could still be in bed. I sat up slowly, and just held my head in my hands, wondering how I was ever going to clean up all of the mess. I felt like I had been run over by a bus, and I probably looked like it as well. Then I spotted the note on the coffee table amongst the mess. The note was from James.

THIS MESS BETTER BE CLEANED UP BEFORE I GET HOME. I EXPECT YOU TO BE HERE, AND HAVE DINNER WAITING.

Seriously? I actually laughed out loud, and then cried out when it hurt to laugh. I couldn't believe his bloody nerve. Have his dinner waiting? I think not!

Not trusting him at all I still got up and walked around the apartment, making sure that he wasn't home. He wasn't, unless he was hiding in a closet. Out of complete paranoia I checked the closets just to be sure. He really wasn't home. That was good news. I went to the door and put the chain on. I was sure he could break through it if he wanted to, but at least I would have some warning.

I didn't know where to start, so I made some coffee, and realized I hadn't eaten since yesterday with Tonya. I made some toast, and took the coffee and toast to my desk. I couldn't find a spot to set anything down, so I figured, what the heck, and swept more papers to the floor. This made me laugh again. It wasn't funny, but it was either laugh or cry, and I didn't want to cry anymore. While I was sitting there with my coffee and toast I decided I should take pictures of the destruction he had caused. I would probably never need them, but, at least I would have them, and hopefully he would never know about them.

I turned on my computer, and checked my email. To make the situation worse there was an email from Tom. I ignored it. I actually thought about deleting it, but didn't. I would hate to miss something that could come back to bite me later. There were emails from the adoption group, I would read them later. My friend in British Columbia had sent a couple as well. I decided I wasn't in the mood for email right then, and closed the program.

I opened up my internet browser, and saw the Google homepage. I was tempted to type in "Luke Clare", but remembered something Elliot had said to me. He said that he didn't know how computer literate James was, but that it was easy enough for anyone to install a program that copied every keystroke into a file that could be accessed later. I didn't know if he knew how to do that, but Elliot had told me in detail how to find out if there was a keystroke logger on the computer. I checked, and sure enough, he had installed something. I didn't know if I should delete the program, or just not do anything on the computer that would tip him off. I decided that I would just do a couple searches like I normally would have done on a Sunday afternoon, and then I decided against that too. He would most definitely check his program, and would see that I had been on the computer and not cleaning up. I closed the browser and decided that a hot shower was in order. Maybe that would energize me a little.

I did feel a little more capable of tackling the mess when I emerged from the bathroom, and started in the bedroom. I knew the living room would be the worst since it was a lot of papers, so I was leaving it until last.

I got the bedroom straightened up, and with all the pain I felt exhausted. I just wanted to crawl under the covers and sleep till next week. Or at least until this nightmare was over. But I stopped myself from lying down, fearful that I would fall asleep and not get the living room cleaned up. I didn't think I would be able to get through all the papers, and get them reorganized, but if I managed to get them all picked up and put in a drawer to go through later I would be satisfied. As for dinner, I sure didn't feel like doing anything for him, but, knew that I had better. So I took some chicken out of the freezer and threw it in the slow cooker with some potatoes and carrots. It wasn't much, but it was better than what I imagined the consequences would be.

Before I started on the living room I decided I should call Tonya. She answered so quickly it was as if she had been holding the phone, waiting for it to ring. That wasn't far from the truth I found out. She had been worrying all day, but didn't want to call in case James was home. I told her almost everything that had happened the night before, all but the rape. I just couldn't say it. She wanted to come over, but I thought it best that she didn't. I would call her later if I could, or try to get over to her house. If I couldn't today, then maybe tomorrow. I didn't think I would be going to work the rest of the week, not after seeing my face in the mirror. So after talking to her I started on the living room. I was doing okay until I got to where my adoption file was. He had ripped it up into tiny pieces. I was so angry I wanted to scream. He didn't want me, or so he said last night, but he didn't want me out of his grasp either. He wanted to isolate me from everyone, and control every aspect of my life. What he didn't know is that when I gave Elliot the notes I had on him, I gave him the originals of any information I had on my adoption, along with some other important papers. I don't know why, but I had the feeling I needed to have them out of the house, safe from his reach. I was glad now that I had. He may have thought he had complete control, but he didn't. Knowing that gave me a little bit of strength, knowing I had my secrets too, secrets that he couldn't do a thing about.

Once I had everything picked up and everything back in its rightful place I made a cup of tea, and sat on the couch in the peace and quiet. It was about 4 p.m. by then. I had the feeling it wouldn't be peaceful around here much longer. Since he wanted dinner waiting for him, I assumed that meant he would be home at dinner time. I waited and waited, and finally at 7 p.m. I ate without him. I left the rest in the slow cooker on low. I was sure when he came home he would make me get it for him, even though there was no reason he couldn't do it himself. I went to bed shortly after 8 p.m., and tried to read a book. I couldn't concentrate on the book, and the next thing I knew he was standing over me. I was so startled when I looked up and saw him I jumped and gasped. I tried to look at the clock to see what time it was, but it hurt too much to turn my head that way, so I just laid there looking at him. Waiting for whatever it was that was coming next. He brought his hand out from behind his back, and while I was preparing for the blow, I realized he had flowers. What a joke. Was a bouquet of flowers supposed to make it all better? I knew better than to say that, and just said thank you instead. He said you're welcome, and walked out of the room. I was getting up, figuring I had to go get his dinner, and possibly even cut his meat for him, but I heard him banging around in the kitchen. He was actually putting the flowers in water, and then he went on to get his own dinner. I was dumbfounded. I had heard of this of course, man beats woman, brings her flowers, and expects her to be so grateful that all is forgiven. Only to have the cycle repeat endlessly until the woman either leaves or he kills her. Did he really think I was going to fall for that? Well, I wasn't going to tell him that I could see through him, just to keep the peace. But I really did see right through his ploy.

I got up and went to the kitchen. He was sitting at the table eating, and didn't acknowledge me at all. I got a drink of water, and went back to bed. I had nothing to say to him. I fell asleep almost immediately, and, in spite of the pain, physical and emotional, I slept straight through until the next morning.

Chapter 27

I got up the next morning, feeling a little better than the day before, but still incredibly sore. My head was clearer though, and I was ready to come up with a plan to get James out of my life for good. I wanted to talk to Elliot and Tonya, and Kim and Tina, my two best friends, and get their input. Other than a little phone contact I hadn't seen Kim or Tina, but I had told them both that I hoped to get out to meet up with them either Thursday or Friday night. Today was Thursday, and I was ready to get together with them. I knew they were going to be horrified by the sight of me, because I was too when I looked in the mirror. I did look like a raccoon with the black eyes, and as hard as I tried, I couldn't cover up all the other bruises and scrapes. Thankfully nothing was broken, and I was still here to see another day. But this couldn't continue. I needed to get rid of him as soon as was humanly possible.

I was alone again that morning, and took advantage of that time to call Kim and Tina, and make plans to get together that night, as long as I could get out. I made sure to let them know that if I didn't make it, he was more than likely home. That was going to be the only reason I wouldn't go. He didn't like me having any friends, and if I made a move to go out I was sure he would fly off the handle again. While talking to Kim I mentioned Elliot and Tanya, and she told me to get them out with us as well, and together the five of us could surely come up with a plan of attack.

I called Tonya at home, and she wanted us all to meet at her house, since the boys would be home, which would mean having to find a babysitter. I was sure that Kim and Tina would be fine with that. They had all met at least once over the last few months. I explained to her the reasoning behind me not showing up, if that should be the case. She knew that Elliot would be sure I got out of the house, even if he had to come and get me. So I called Kim and Tina again, and gave them the address of the house.

With that done I took my time getting showered and dressed, and planned to just relax the rest of the day. When I got out of the bathroom, James was home, sitting on the couch, trying his best to look forlorn. I wasn't fooled. I went to my desk, and started looking through more papers that he had thrown around. I felt like I sat there for hours with him just staring at me, not talking. The silence was deafening, and the tension in the room was very thick.

He cleared his throat, and said, "Emma, are you okay?"

I just scoffed at him, and didn't reply.

"I'm so very sorry Emma. I just lost control, it's never happened before. You can't imagine how bad I feel about all of this," he said.

"You just lost control?" I asked him. "How do you just lose control, and then trash my apartment, rape me, and nearly kill me?" I just stared at him in disbelief. I was going to throw in that he was damn lucky he wasn't sitting in jail, but I didn't need a repeat of the other night and decided not to push it any further right now.

"I don't know how it happens. I do know why I was so mad though. I know you're cheating on me," he replied.

I felt like my jaw hit the floor. "How in the hell could I be cheating on you? You don't want me going anywhere unless it's to work. No, let me rephrase that, you don't let me go anywhere. I can't live like this, and it's time you left." I was trying to control my anger. I was terrified of him, and I was sure he knew it.

"What do you mean leave? For tonight? So you can go see your new boyfriend and cry to him? Or leave for good? Either way, it doesn't matter, because I will not be leaving tonight and I will certainly not be moving out. I have nowhere to go, and since I live here you can't kick me out. This is my home too. So if you don't want to be around me, you move." He sat there looking so smug, thinking that he had won.

"I will not be leaving, this is my home. This was my sanctuary at one time, and I am hoping once you are out of my life for good it will be again. I will go to any lengths necessary to have you forcibly removed if that's what is necessary." I was losing my cool, and I needed to calm down and think about what I was saying. His face was going dark, and he was getting that look that had scared me so much the other night. I wasn't sure I would live this time if he beat me again. I wasn't sure I had the fight left in me. I had to get away from him, so I went into the kitchen. I was starting to cry, and I was shaking with fear.

He walked into the kitchen and grabbed my arm. It hurt so much, he was squeezing so hard, right on top of bruises he left Tuesday night. I tried to pull my arm away, but he had such a tight grip on it I couldn't get free. My whole body was vibrating with fear, and I could feel the colour drain out of my face. He gave me a hard shove towards the wall, and stood there glaring at me. I was cornered, and terrified. But I would not beg him not to hurt me. He hadn't completely robbed me of all my pride. I stood there, waiting for the attack. After a minute or so he turned and walked out of the kitchen. I almost collapsed with relief, my knees buckled, but I managed to get to a chair. I didn't know if he was coming back or not. I could hear him walking around in the living room.

When he came back in the kitchen he had his back pack. For a few seconds I was hopeful for the first time in days. I thought he was going to leave. I couldn't believe he had given in. Then he set the back pack on the chair, and opened it. My elation quickly turned to fear again. I knew what was coming.

"Do you know what I discovered the other day? I discovered that someone had been in my back pack, and had been going through my papers," he said. He paused for a moment, and then continued on. "Do you know how I know someone had done this?"

I was guessing at this point that his questions were really just rhetorical. He wasn't giving me time to answer them anyway.

"I know someone went through them because I know exactly what order they were in. They have all been in the very same order for a long time now, and I put them that way purposefully so that I would know if someone had gone through them," his voice was getting angrier and angrier sounding with every word. "Now, I don't want to just assume that it was you, but since I left it here the other night, I have no other choice but to think that. I don't let it out of my sight normally, but you made me so mad that I left without it." He paused here like he was thinking of what to say next.

I just sat there, knowing that anything I could say would just enrage him, and I had found out what happens when he gets really mad. I really wanted to confront him with what I knew, but I was too scared to. So for now I just sat and listened.

"I don't know why you would feel the need to go through my belongings. I don't go through yours."

I had to force myself not to laugh out loud. I wanted to ask him if he would like to see the pictures I had taken of the results of him "not going through mine". But, I didn't. I knew he wasn't done talking, and I was not going to add any more fuel to his fire.

"So," he went on, "I have decided that you can't be trusted, and from now on you will go to work, you will come home, and anywhere else you go, I will go. Just remember what happens when you do something behind my back. Next time you won't look as good as you do now." And having had his say he walked out to the living room and turned on the television.

I was fuming. I didn't know what to do, and I didn't know how I was going to get out of the house that evening. I stayed in the kitchen, crying silently; not wanting to let on to him how much he had gotten under my skin. He might take everything else from me, but my tears and sorrow were mine. I would not let him have those.

I started to make some dinner, all the while trying to figure out how to get out of the house later. I still hadn't come up with anything before we ate. I had pretty much resigned myself to not getting out of there that night.

Chapter 28

We ate dinner in silence, and the tension was so thick it was suffocating. I cleaned up and started trying to figure out how to get out of the house. I thought to myself that maybe I should let him follow me, and deliver him right into the lion's den, let Elliot get a hold of him, and let the chips fall where they may. I quickly dismissed that idea. I would not force this drama on anyone else, and James was so unpredictable I had no way of knowing how he would react.

I was sitting in my window seat trying to read a book, while he was stretched out on the couch with the television blaring. I did ask him to turn the volume down at one point, and James being James, he turned it up. I just shook my head and went back to my book. I wasn't really concentrating on it anyway; I was still trying to figure a way out for tonight. I wasn't coming up with anything that seemed reasonable. Not that reasonable lived here anymore.

The time for me to leave came and went, and I resigned myself to the fact that I wouldn't be going out. I was frustrated, and angry with myself that I didn't just stand up to him and go.

Just as I was getting the courage up to make a move to go out the phone rang. It was Tonya, but of course he answered the phone, and then stood over me the whole time we talked.

"Emma?" Tonya asked. "Are you okay?"

"Yeah," I said. "Just relaxing after dinner, trying to read a book."

"You aren't coming over then?" she asked.

"No, I am not going to work tomorrow," I replied. "I'm just not feeling up to it yet, and James thinks I shouldn't go anywhere yet"

Thankfully she caught on to what I was trying to say but wasn't able to say, and asked me if she should send Elliot over. Or if they should all come over.

"Sure, that sounds good," I replied. "We can do that Monday when I get back to work."

"Okay," she said, "we're all heading over there right now. See you soon."

"Take care Tonya, thanks for calling," I said and hung up the phone. I picked up my book and waited at the window. I knew they wouldn't be long getting here, and I was trying not to let my anxiety show over the ensuing confrontation. I wasn't sure if I was hiding it well or not, but he didn't say anything to me, just went back to the couch and his television show. All I could do now was wait.

Chapter 29

I was antsy, but I forced myself to sit in that window seat, waiting for the car to pull into the driveway. I didn't want to get up and do anything that would make him suspicious that something was going on.

Within fifteen minutes, which felt like fifteen hours to me, they were there. I gave a small smile out the window, knowing they could see me sitting there, but made no move to get up.

When the knock on the door came James jumped off the couch to get to the door first. I just let him go, but I was worried that he would meet a fist when he opened it. He didn't, Elliot was at the back of the bunch. Kim and Tina just pushed past him without a word, and walked into the apartment. Their faces said it all. They were shocked by the look of my face, and then the pity started to show. They both just walked over to me, and hugged me as tight as they could, but gently, without causing me more pain.

James was at the door trying to keep Elliot from entering, which was okay since I was leaving with them. James threatened something about following me, which was an empty threat because I was taking my car, so he wouldn't have any way to follow us. I got my coat and purse, and started to walk out the door. James grabbed my arm, and in a tone that chilled me, I heard Elliot tell him to get his hands off me. James actually backed down, which just confirmed for me that he really was a coward. He felt like a big man beating on a woman, but when push came to shove with a man, he turned and ran with his tail between his legs.

I got in my car, and Kim and Tina rode with me to Elliot and Tonya's house. While I was embarrassed to have them see me like this, it was a huge relief to be out of that apartment, and away from James. I had reservations about what my place may look like when I returned, but I had to remember that things could be replaced, lives couldn't. The girls were so concerned, and so outraged, and, even though they wouldn't admit it, scared for me. I loved them for their concern, but I didn't want them to worry about me like they were. It was unfair to have them stressed out as well. I was carrying enough stress for all of us. And now it was time for action. It was time to come up with a plan to get him out of my life for good.

Chapter 30

When we were all settled in at Elliot and Tonya's house we broke out a couple bottles of wine. Of course the foremost thing on everyone's minds was getting James out of my apartment for good. But we just talked and tried to relax first while we all had a glass of wine. My eyes kept welling up with tears, just knowing how far these people were willing to go to keep me safe, and how I would do the same for any one of them. Once we all seemed to be relaxed a little I filled Tina and Kim in on everything that I had found out on Sunday by going through his back pack. The double identities, the fact that he was on welfare, everything. Elliot then told them what he had found. James did have parents that were alive and living in New Jersey, as well as a brother and sister in New Jersey as well.

Since I had seen Elliot he had found out more information about James, and had also made inquiries with the police as to what I can do to have him evicted from my apartment. It was as I had figured, since he wasn't on the lease, and didn't use the address as his own, I could have him removed by the police anytime if he wouldn't leave, and they would trespass him right then and there. After that was done I would go and have a restraining order put against him. I wanted everyone there to do the same, as well as one for work. I could not put it past James to stalk any one of the four of them, or all of them. He seemed to think he had some kind of ownership over me, and because he felt that entitlement, he would think he could do anything he wanted to find me.

They all agreed; it cost nothing to take out a restraining order, so they would all get one. That way there was some recourse for each one of them and their families if he started harassing them. I felt a little better knowing they would do that, knowing deep down that it probably wouldn't scare him off, but, if the police were called, they might show up a little quicker when they were told there was a restraining order in effect.

The welfare office was not much help to Elliot. Basically we could report him, or not, but it would be better if he was reported. Well of course that's what they would say, but, it was good to know there weren't a lot of hoops to jump through there.

I hadn't told them that James had accused me of cheating on him. That gave everyone a good laugh, knowing the situation with Tom and how crushed I had been. There was no way I would ever have cheated on anyone, before or after Tom. It was a respect thing. If you want out to be with someone else, there are ways to get out. You don't have to cheat on anyone. There is no excuse for it.

Now to come up with a plan to get him out. I really just wanted to make it as easy for everyone as possible. I wanted to call the police, have them escort him out, and then trespass him right then and there. If there was any violence they would be there to take care of it, and hopefully no one would be hurt. Everyone thought that would be a good plan. It was just a matter of someone being there with me when it was done. Of course they all wanted to be there, which was okay with me, so basically any night after dinner would work. I would just call one of them and let them know, and they would let the others know.

I was still going to work for the answering service part of the company. I thought it might be fun, and once I had James out of the apartment, shift work would be no problem. So that was settled that night as well. As soon as he was out, I would start training. Until then I would just stay with the receptionist position. I was just thankful that not a lot of people came to the office. Most meetings were off site, so the foot traffic was a relatively low volume. Mostly just people that worked there and I was going to have to face them eventually, so there was no time like Monday, right?

We never said what Monday that would be. It certainly wasn't going to be the following Monday. We didn't know that then though.

Chapter 31

The rest of the evening we just tried to have some fun, they tried to take my mind off everything. It was just nice to be out with friends, and not have to worry about what he was going to do. Going home, however, worried me a little. I was hoping he would just be gone, but I knew he wouldn't, since he had nowhere else to go. I tried to keep up a strong front when I was leaving Elliot and Tonya's house, but I could hear the quiver in my voice, and I'm sure they could as well. I was hoping I had stayed out late enough for him to be asleep when I got home. My heart sunk a little when I saw lights on, but he could still be asleep on the couch.

I sat in the car for a few minutes, just getting my head together, and finally couldn't put off going in. I walked slowly to the door, and opened it. The chain was on. I knocked on the door, and I could hear the television going. I knew he was in the living room, and I knew that he wouldn't be sleeping. I just had such a feeling of dread right then, I should have turned around and walked back out. But I didn't.

I knocked a little louder, and finally heard him coming to the door. He wouldn't take the chain off. He had that evil look on his face again, and I knew it wasn't going to be pretty when I did get in. I asked him to let me in. He refused. I started to walk back out to the car, and all of a sudden the door flew open and he was running at me. I was able to turn and run past him, but I didn't get the door locked in time. He burst in through the door, accusing me of sleeping with Elliot and claiming his wife and my two friends were covering it up. I asked him if he even heard what he was saying. His wife was covering it up? That made no sense, but then I should have known that common sense occupied no place in his mind. I was trying so hard not to laugh at the sheer idiocy of it all. But I couldn't help myself. I let out a little laugh. That was the beginning of the end.

By that time I was standing in the bedroom door, and he ran at me with all the force he had. He hit me so hard that I flew backwards, and cracked my head on the bed frame. I was on the floor and he started kicking me. Somehow I had to get away from him, and the only way out I could see was under the bed. I didn't know I could move so quickly. I was under the bed with one roll, and trying to get to the other side. He was reaching under the bed, trying to grab me. I managed to get out the other side, and grabbed the phone. I didn't get a chance to dial before he was on me again, and ripped the phone out of my hand, then the phone cord out of the wall. I was trying to scramble to get to the living room phone, but he beat me to it. I was completely trapped now. I was terrified. He was making a sound that sounded like a growling, mad dog. It was like he had completely lost his mind. He lunged at me, and got hold of me. He just started pummeling me. Over and over and over. With all the hurt and pain from the first beating he had given me, I just wanted to die. I was in incredible pain. I think I gave up at that point. I just had no fight left in me. He was calling me all kinds of filthy names, and accusing me of the most ridiculous things, and all I could do was cry and beg him to stop. He didn't stop. Somehow we had made it into the hallway in the apartment, and the only spot where there was no carpet covering the cement floors. Just tiles. Thin tiles at that. It didn't matter what was on the floor, it wasn't going to protect me any. The last thing I remember is him pounding my head into that floor, I remember two or three times, and then, mercifully, I finally lost consciousness. What he did after that I have no idea, and never will know for sure.

A neighbour had heard my screams, and cries, and called the police. She lived above me. The police had to pull him off me according to what I was later told. He was close to killing me. I almost became a statistic that night. My body, my brain, could not have taken much more. Maybe one or two more hits that would have, at the very least, caused irreparable damage.

I had angels watching over me that night. I had an earthly angel in that woman that called the police, and other angels watching over me in my unconscious state. By the grace of God I am here today, and have very few residual effects.

For the next four days I was I in a coma. As most people will probably know, there is no way to tell the full extent of any brain trauma until a person is conscious. So for four days I lay there unconscious, with worried friends keeping vigil at my bedside. The most hurtful thing I found out after waking up was that one of the girls called my adoptive mother the night it happened, and she didn't care. She never came to the hospital, and to this day I believe she never told my father. I know he would have been at my bedside as well, if he had known. It's been fourteen years since I have seen my parents. I will never forgive her for making my dad choose sides. Her or me. How was that fair? He had to live with her, so his choice, no matter how painful, was obvious.

My friends were so elated to see me awake, but I still needed a lot of rest, and the pain killers were so strong that I was in a fog for at least the next week. I don't remember any of it. Occasionally I have what I think are memories of that time, but I don't know if they are my memories, or if I am remembering what they told me happened.

Unbelievably I had no broken bones. A lot of serious bruising, and because he had kicked me around as well, my insides hurt. I hurt down to the very core of my being. But I would heal. The biggest worry was the brain trauma. I still have some memory problems to this day, and thankfully, I have no memory other than that first few minutes of that horrible night.

I have trouble with putting my thoughts into words sometimes, more so when I am tired. In the fourteen years since it happened that has never changed. It's not that bad really, when I consider the other end of the scale. I could have died. I could have remained in a coma for the rest of my life. I could have come out of the coma and essentially been a vegetable. So the little things that I have to put up with now are a blessing in disguise it seems. Those things that are still with me remind me how lucky I was, how precious life is, and how to not let a man take advantage of me in any way ever again.

It took me a long time to remember the events of that night before I got home, and when it finally came back to me I joked that we wasted all that time coming up with a plan to get him out of my life. We wasted that time on him, when we could have been having fun. I guess that's my defense, I have always used humour to cover my hurt.

Needless to say, I have not seen James since that night. I accomplished my goal in a roundabout sort of way. I got him out of my apartment, and I got my sanctuary back, eventually.

I remained in the hospital for about three weeks, and recuperated at home for another two weeks before I tried to go back to work part time. It was hard, I won't lie. But I did it. I could only work a couple of hours a day at first, and very quickly I realized I was not ready to be back at work. I talked to Elliot about it, and told him I had to resign because I couldn't do the work, and they needed someone that could. Begrudgingly he accepted my resignation, but called it a medical leave of absence. Whenever I was ready to come back to work, my job was there. What a true friend I had in him, but more importantly, has there ever been a more understanding boss? Not in my life.

I felt like I was finally going to be able to heal, physically, emotionally, and mentally, thanks to Elliot's reassurance that my job was there, no matter if it took me two weeks, two months, or two years to feel ready to be back. I certainly hoped it wouldn't be years, in fact, I hoped it wouldn't take me many months to feel ready to be back.

Chapter 32

With that horrible chapter of my life over, I had lots of time at home alone. I had been alone before, so that wasn't the hard part. The hard part was the nightmares. I didn't want to give up my apartment because I really did love living there. And I refused to let him take one more thing away from me. So I stayed there. But for the first week after I was released from the hospital I had someone with me every night. My friends, I could not thank them enough. I was prepared to stay alone, but they wouldn't hear of it. Daylight hours were fine. It was the dark that scared me. The shadows. My imagination making me believe that there was someone hiding in the shadows. So every night I had someone on my couch to keep the boogie man away. After being home for a week I felt like I was imposing on them, and I insisted that I wanted to try it alone. The first night was hard. I woke up with every little noise I heard. But I made it through the night. I was so proud of myself. It was another small achievement for me. My apartment was going to become my sanctuary again. It would take some time, but it would happen.

Before I returned home my friends had gone in and cleaned everything up, had my phone lines fixed, and scoured the apartment to make sure that there was no trace of what James had done to me left. Being that I couldn't remember most of what happened, that was a big deal to me. I didn't have to go in and confront the mess, and wonder what exactly had happened. The good thing about James being taken away by the police that night was that his back pack was left behind. I didn't want anything of his, but, I did decide that maybe I would keep all that paperwork, and just in case he ever tried to contact me again, I would have the ammunition this time. Eventually I destroyed it all; there was no need to keep it. In order to move on I had to be rid of it all. There was nothing in my life now that reminded me at all of James, and in time his face became a blur. I still have one picture of him buried with my pictures, just in case he should ever decide he needs to find me, I will have a picture to show the police should the occasion arise. To date it never has, and hopefully never will.

It was time to move on, and start anew once again. I wasn't sure what was in store for me, until the day I was looking for something in a desk drawer, and I came across my Adoption Order. That was my mission now. That was what I was going to dedicate myself to. When you come that close to losing your life, your priorities become much clearer. I needed to work on the search for my birth family. I needed to find my birth mother and brother. Hopefully they were the pot of gold at the end of the rainbow for me.

Chapter 33

I spent the first few weeks trying to readjust one more time to my new life. It wasn't easy. In less than six months I had had two relationships end badly. One a marriage that I thought would last forever, and the other a mistake I knew I was making from the very beginning.

So the first thing I had to do to get one step closer to the end of this journey was forgive myself for the huge mistake I had made with James. Easier said than done. Everywhere I looked in my apartment I was confronted with memories of him. I tried so very hard to remember the good times, but I finally had to admit to myself that there were no good times, no honest times. I knew it wasn't right for me to be in the relationship from the very beginning, but yet, I had let it continue. I knew then, and especially now, it was wrong. All wrong.

I was having trouble even trying to forgive myself while I was still in this apartment, seeing visions of what had happened everywhere.

I did have a good laugh in those first few days alone. I realized that the only place, the one and only space that he had not violated in the apartment was my window seat. I wondered, only for about five seconds, if that had been a sign of some kind of warped respect from him towards me. That was the moment I laughed out loud, and in that moment I realized that was the most honest moment I had had where James was concerned. He had zero respect for me, and, more than likely he had no respect for any woman. How I wished I could warn any woman he became involved with in the future, but I didn't want to know where he was or what he was doing. I had to let go of everything James. Physically, James was gone from my life, but spiritually, mentally, emotionally, that was the garbage that had to go. I wasn't sure that I could do that here, around all the memories. It was difficult trying to stay positive, and trying to keep the worry off my friends' faces. I knew that they worried, even though they would never admit it. They were my biggest support system, and I just couldn't let them down. They deserved better than that, they deserved to have the Emma they knew back. The Emma that wasn't broken, feeling unfixable.

Since I was not able to work, I had a lot of time at home alone. I needed a lot of rest, but as I got stronger each day I was able to spend more and more time doing the things that I wanted to do. Namely, starting my search for my birth family all over again. I hadn't gotten very far before James entered my life, so it was easy to catch myself up. I still had my notes, and I went back to all the websites I had registered on, made sure my information was correct, and started looking for new sites. At that point that was all I knew how to do. Register on a site hoping that my birth mother, or another member of my birth family, was looking for me. But I didn't think that anyone else knew about me since my mother had me in Ontario, and then had gone back to Newfoundland sometime after she gave me up. So chances were that if she wasn't looking, there would not be anyone else that was. But I had to do something and right then that was all I knew how to do.

After registering for what seemed like hundreds of websites I started reading all the information I could on other searches. I wanted to get ideas of how to go about it from other people's experiences. I was not naïve enough to think that what worked for one person would work for me too. Like I had said before, there are as many stories about searching as there are adoptees and family members searching. I also read a lot of stories about reunions. There were great reunions, there were mediocre reunions, and there were awful reunions. Some adoptees were welcomed with open arms by their birth families. Some adoptees had contact with a member of their birth family that was great at first, then either dwindled to no more contact, or turned into an awful downward spiraling story of people falling apart, and wishing they had never found each other. Some adoptees were rejected a second time by their birth mothers. I had to go into this search hoping for somewhere between a good and a great reunion, because if I dwelled on the bad at that point I would not have bothered to search.

I had probably close to five hundred emails to go through when I got home. Most were not relevant to me or my search. There were quite a few from Emily in British Columbia. Some had info on what she thought may be my birth family. Some were just to say hi, and check in on me. I was back in contact with her, and we continued to get to know each other, although I didn't tell her what had just happened to me at that point. I wasn't ready to let anyone in yet, and that wasn't a story that could be told lightly.

So we chatted on the internet at least once a day, even if it was just to say hi, and touch base. Very quickly she started to be someone that I could confide in, and sometimes it's much easier to confide in someone on the computer because you can't see that person's eyes, and see their reactions to anything you say. Many people over the years have said that they have fallen in love over the internet, and it was a deeper kind of love than had they met in person first. There was no preconceived notion about appearance; all you had was words, and getting to know someone that way people seem to have a deeper connection. When they do finally meet in person appearances mean nothing because they have already gotten to know the person from the inside out. Most people would say it's a deeper passion, and that they are so glad they met their significant other online, and not in a bar, or the grocery store, or wherever single people meet each other.

Having my adoption search as a project helped me start to move on past James because I kept myself busy with the search. If there was a time that I started to think about him, and didn't want to, I would go read more information online. If I started to feel alone and lonely, I would go read more information online. I would chat with my new friend Emily in British Columbia. She became more and more like a mom to me, and eventually I would begin to call her Mom. She had four children, all close to my age, two older, two younger. She said I fit right in the middle for a reason. In fact, meeting her was to become one of the most wonderful blessings I could have had in my life.

But I was still stuck. As hard as I tried I just couldn't get past James, and the pain that he had caused me, in this, my sanctuary.

Chapter 34

Knowing that I was never going to get past James staying here, and knowing that I had a job to come back to, I decided there was nothing that could heal me, body and soul, more than a road trip. I made arrangements with Tina, Kim, Elliot and Tonya to look after my place for me, which wasn't much of a job really. Check the mail every few days, go in and water my plants occasionally, and make sure everything is okay inside.

So I loaded my car up and took off. I decided to head west, and go through the United States as a shortcut, instead of the long drive through Ontario. Crossing the border was a little nerve wracking, but once I was through I felt free.

Since I had no place to be, I had called a couple of friends that I had gotten to know online. They were both in Oregon, and after making the phone calls, only then did it sink in that I had decided to drive across the country. I had a sense of how life was in the United States, having lived there for a few years, but I had no idea what life was like in Oregon, and on the west coast in general. Where I had lived in Pennsylvania things had really not been that much different than Canada.

I took my time driving across the states towards the west coast. The first night I stayed in Ann Arbor, Michigan. I wasn't rich, so I certainly wasn't staying at anything upscale, but I was not going to stay in a roach infested motel either. Motel 6 seemed reasonable, so that's where I stayed that first night. It was still early enough in the day for me to explore, have a nice dinner, and get a good rest before heading out in the morning, so that is exactly what I did.

I woke up in the morning feeling quite rested. It was the first time in weeks that I had felt that way. So I packed up the car again, and headed in the direction of Chicago. Once I got there I had to decide on one of three routes. I would figure that out when I got there. I still had the cell phone that Elliot and Tonya had given me, so the first time I stopped for a rest I called Tonya to let her know all was well, where I was, and to be totally honest, just to hear a comforting voice from home. Leaving for a while was truly the best decision, but I still missed my friends, and I felt a little lonely being such a long way from home.

It was about a four hour drive from Ann Arbor to Chicago, but I took my time and made it in about five hours. This got me to the Chicago area around noon. Lunch time. Traffic was insane everywhere I looked. Perfect time to stop for another rest, and have some lunch, and wait out the lunch rush hour. I sure hoped traffic wasn't this crazy all day long. But it was. I had lots of time to decide what route to take west, and decided on the I-90 West because it looked a little more scenic than any other route. I gathered my courage, and made the trip around Chicago. I honestly had never driven through such traffic, and I don't think I took a breath from the time I got in the car until I was well outside the city and stopped at the first rest area I saw. Chalk one up for Emma. I had conquered one fear, many more to go, but one was a step in the right direction.

I stopped early that day, in a town called Ontario, near the Illinois/Wisconsin border. Being in Ontario, though not my Ontario, made me feel a little less lonely somehow. It's silly how the mind works sometimes. I went for a walk, checking out the town, and then touched base with people at home again. It was another early night, and another early morning departure, but, amazingly, I still felt well rested.

Chapter 35

If you have never had the opportunity to drive cross country, I believe that everyone should have that chance at least once in their lives. Whether alone, as I was, or with friends or family, stopping at new places, and reflecting on life, my experience was that I was able to find the real me again. I was pleasantly surprised.

When I crossed the border into Oregon two days later, I was feeling strong and confident again, ready to face life head on. I don't think I could have picked a better time to take this journey. It was fall, my favourite time of the year. The trees were in full colour, and everywhere I walked there were crunchy leaves, my favourite sound of fall. When I found crunchy, dry leaves I was like a child, making all the noise I could, and going out of my way to walk through them. Everywhere I looked there was red, orange, yellow leaves on the trees. When I could I stopped and took in all the beauty that nature had to offer, I took pictures, and enjoyed the cool, crisp air of fall.

I was really starting to see what the west coast had to offer, and knowing I was getting closer to the ocean mile by mile, I felt more peace coming over me. Water had always had a calming effect on me, and I needed that serenity in my life. During the drive I had done a lot of soul searching, and realized that I had a lot of big life decisions to make. To me it was easier to make these kinds of decisions away from home, and all those influences. Not that they were bad influences, but I had to be clear headed, and dedicated to making the choices and sticking to them. Every day I was a little closer to having my mind made up about where I wanted to go with my life.

I met up with Josh and Karen, the friends I had met online, that evening for dinner. We had a lot of laughs, and they seemed like good people. Normal and down to earth. Josh said he was

From Lost To Found

available the next day to show me the sights in Hermiston, and around the area, but wondered if it wouldn't be easier to stay at his place that night, and get an early start in the morning. Really? It took me not even one full second to say no. I was not getting myself into that kind of situation or any danger here, miles away from my safety. Right then I made the decision that he didn't need to know what motel I was staying at. I realized this was my fear taking over, and that hopefully he was just being nice, not expecting anything more than friendship, but I still wasn't going to put myself in that position. This time I listened to the bells ringing inside my head. They weren't loud, but they were ringing gently to remind me to use my head, to err on the side of caution.

I was shaking my head about that whole conversation when I got back to my motel room after dinner. But I had to be proud of myself for the fact that I hadn't put myself into any kind of uncomfortable or potentially dangerous position just so that I wouldn't hurt his feelings. That was a definite change for me. I was used to trying to make everyone else happy, and not worrying about myself. Things seemed like they might be changing for me, in a good way.

The next morning I was up early and ready to head out exploring. I had lots of time to go find somewhere to have breakfast, gas up my car, and meet Josh at the restaurant we had been to the night before. We spent the morning driving around the area, and although it was beautiful country, there wasn't much there to really excite me. The mountains were beautiful, and I decided I would drive up into them the next day alone, but for this day I had had enough sight-seeing, and dropped Josh off to get his truck. We were all meeting for dinner that night, and I had realized that seeing Josh again was going to be enough time spent with him for me.

I arrived at the restaurant that night and to my surprise Josh was there alone. I was hoping that Karen was just running late, but I had an uneasy feeling in the pit of my stomach. I asked him where Karen was, and he just said she couldn't make it. So we had dinner, but it wasn't really comfortable or relaxing for me. Josh suggested that we go back to his place, and my answer was a definitive no. I explained to him that I was not looking for any kind of relationship with anyone, it wasn't just him. He knew what I had gone through with James, but yet he seemed offended that I didn't see him as anything more than a friend. At that moment calling him a friend seemed like a stretch. We parted ways outside the restaurant, although it wasn't very friendly. I sat in my car until he was gone, but I still felt really uneasy. I felt like I was being watched. It may have been my fears coming back, but I just didn't feel good at all, and I hated this feeling. The motel I was staying at had internet access, so I decided to check my email. There was nothing important, so I quickly emailed everyone back home to let them know how I was doing, and what my plan was. I was going to mention Josh and his attitude, but I knew that would only cause them to worry, and I didn't want them to do that. I would tell them when I got home again.

Still feeling uneasy when I got back into my room I decided that maybe I should look at some other options. I took out my road map, and saw that I really wasn't all that far from Portland, considering how far I had already come. The decision to leave Hermiston that night was easy, it was a matter of where to go. Portland was over a three hour drive, which I could do, and that got me much closer to the ocean. Between Portland and Hermiston there was a town on the map called The Dalles. Just the name sounded interesting, so I thought I would drive that far to start with, and if I thought it was interesting enough I would stay there tonight, and drive on to Portland the next day. So once again I packed up the car, and was ready to head out again on my adventure. Just as I was leaving something caught my eye in the back of the parking lot. It was a truck, just like Josh's truck, and I instantly started to shake. I was thrown back in time to when James was following me everywhere I went. I was scared and angry at the same time. To my credit though, I was more angry than scared this time. That was a change. Before I had been terrified, and my anger took a back seat. Maybe I was growing, even though at that moment I didn't feel like it.

Should I drive to the back of the lot and confront him? Maybe it wasn't him after all. I decided to leave, and start driving towards my destination. I would pull over at the first place I felt was safe if I felt that I was being followed.

I didn't have to drive more than a couple of blocks to realize my instinct was dead on. Josh was in the truck, right behind me. I pulled into the first variety store that I saw, hoping they would be open, and there would be people around should it get ugly. I was praying it wouldn't, but I knew I had to confront him.

Of course he pulled in behind me, but pulled into the back of the parking lot, almost behind the building, I guess he assumed I didn't know he was there. Apparently to him I appeared to be brainless.

I walked to the corner of the building, and just leaned against the wall, waiting for him to get out of his truck and come to me. I was not going to go back where he was parked, where people couldn't see us. Finally he came over to me, and tried to look all sheepish and apologetic. I didn't fall for it, not one bit. I guess I had hardened my heart some because I would have fallen for that before.

I asked him why he was following me. Why had he followed me to the motel? Let alone why he had followed me leaving the motel. I was shaking I was so angry, but I was still able to get the conversation started without screaming at him. His response was that he thought there was more between us, he guessed. I just laughed. I told him there was absolutely nothing between us, and that I couldn't believe he thought there was. How could there be? We had only met a couple of days beforehand, but yet he had all these feelings for me? It was so ridiculous that it bordered on absurd. I asked him politely to stop following me, that I would like him to leave first, and I would like him to drive in the opposite direction of me. He actually obliged me. That was the last I ever saw of Josh, and that was just fine with me.

I sat in my car for a few minutes after he left gathering my thoughts. To sit there and dwell on it was not going to do me any good, so I decided to keep on driving. I headed for The Dalles, shaking my head about the whole Josh issue, but also nervously checking my mirror frequently. Thankfully he wasn't behind me, and eventually I stopped looking for him.

I got to The Dalles about two hours later, and found a motel to check into. While checking in I noticed there was a rack of brochures advertising all the things to do in the area, so I grabbed a few that looked interesting and headed for my room to check them out. It turns out that The Dalles is quite historic, and has lots of attractions for tourists. The first thing I noticed was a walking tour, and I thought that would be fun to do. There was also a few museums there to go through, so I thought I may spend a couple of days here sight-seeing. I was so glad that I did. The town was beautiful, and the people were very welcoming. I got back into my happy place there, during the walking tour. The town was rich in history, and the end of the Oregon Trail is marked there.

After the walking tour I decided to take a drive around the area to see the countryside. There is a dam there, which was nice to see, but the most beautiful view was from the Rowena Plateau. There is a stunning view of the Columbia River Gorge, and a hiking trail as well. I walked the trail, taking in all that nature had to offer, and felt very refreshed and relaxed when I finished. I sat for a while and just stared out at the view, really thinking about nothing in particular, and finally realized that I needed to see the ocean. I had seen much of what The Dalles had to offer, so I decided it was time to move on down the road. I consulted the road map again, and spotted a place called Rockaway Beach. For some reason I was drawn to that specific place, and that was where I was headed. It would take me a little over three hours to get there so once again I hit the road, and headed west. I was very excited, knowing I was finally going to see the ocean. I was really hoping I could find a motel close to the ocean, and with a view of the ocean would be even better.

It was late afternoon when I arrived in Rockaway Beach, and the first thing I did was park my car and walk down to the ocean. I was finally there, on the west coast, looking out over the Pacific Ocean. Suddenly I felt very small. I also felt more calm and peaceful than I had in a very long time. This was exactly what my soul needed to begin healing. Right then and there I knew that I had made the right decision. In fact, it felt like home, even though it wasn't home to me. At that point I think I knew that eventually, somehow, some way, I would end up living on the west coast of Canada. That became my goal, to get to where I had my peace.

I spent a few days in Rockaway Beach, just reflecting on my life, and trying to make a concrete plan for the future. I was feeling so rested, and so content with the decisions I had made, and now I knew that this trip was completely worth it. This is what my soul needed. My body needed rest, my mind needed rest, and all of me needed to heal.

I walked around the town a little, but mostly I spent my time at the water, staring out at the ocean, and feeling more and more content each minute. I didn't want to leave, but I knew I had to. I had put it off as long as I possibly could, and made my plan to get back to Ontario. I decided that I was going to drive back through Canada, and see the west coast there. In the back of my mind I still thought that I would end up living on the west coast sometime in the future. I wasn't sure how far in the future, but it was a goal of mine to move there. It would mean leaving home again, but I had done it before and survived, so I knew I could do it again.

Before I left Oregon I emailed another online friend. He lived outside Chicago, and I thought that since I had made this long trek, I should meet him now. The opportunity may never arise again. I gave him my cell phone number and told him to give me a call, and if we decided we wanted to meet we would work out the details then. I never really gave it much thought after that, and headed through Washington State towards Canada. The first day I drove as long as I could, and that got me through Seattle and as far as Bellingham, Washington. I decided to spend the night there, and get up early the next morning so I would be crossing the border sometime in the morning, and maybe it wouldn't be too busy.

After dinner as I was headed back to my room my cell phone rang. It was Michael from Chicago. We had a great conversation, with a lot of laughs, and he felt like someone I had known forever. We decided I would stop and see him on the way back to Ontario, and I could stay as long as I wanted to. I felt more comfortable with him than I had with Josh, and I hoped that our meeting would be a better experience. The only downfall was I was headed back to Chicago again, and I already knew I hated the traffic there. But I would do it, and be fine, I was confident in that.

Chapter 36

I drove east across Canada, marvelling at how beautiful my native land is. From the Pacific Ocean I went through the Rocky Mountains. From the Rockies to Calgary, home of the Calgary Stampede. Then through the prairies, the flat, flat prairies, all the way to Winnipeg, Manitoba. From the west coast to Winnipeg I felt like I had seen three different seasons. The weather on the coast was like summer, snow in the mountains, and the beautiful fall foliage from Calgary to Winnipeg.

During the drive I surprised myself at how settled I felt. I realized I had finally found where I was at peace, and I knew how I was going to attain that peace. All I had to do was move to the west coast. That was my plan. And I had always seen my plans through, maybe not quickly, but eventually.

After a night in Winnipeg, I drove to the border, and crossed into North Dakota. God's country. It was breathtaking. I stopped soon after crossing the border to check my map and stretch my legs. I saw that I would be going through Fargo, North Dakota. One of my favourite movies was Fargo, so it was going to be fun to see the actual city. I wondered if I would recognize any of the town from the movie. I wasn't even sure if the film had actually been made in Fargo, but it was still going to be neat to say I have been to Fargo.

Fargo is on the North Dakota/Minnesota border, and once I was through there I decided to drive on to Minneapolis for the night. I was hoping to find a reasonably priced motel right off the interstate, so that I wouldn't have to go through the city itself. I was lucky enough to find one, and I checked in and headed to my room. I was tired, but I was hungry too, so I had to find some dinner. I was actually close to a truck stop, and we all know that truck stop meals are fabulous. Some of the best home cooking a person can get is truck stop food. It was early evening, and the place was quite busy. I managed to find a booth that wasn't full, and had my dinner there, people watching. I loved to people watch, and wonder what their lives were like.

After dinner I went right back to my room, and decided to call Michael, just to be sure we were still on for the next day. He was excited about it, at least he sounded like he was, and we had another rather long chat on the phone, full of laughs again. I felt very comfortable with him. It was scary. I didn't want to be any more than friends, but in the back of my mind I had this thought that he was such a great guy, we were both single, who knows what could happen? So I had a bit of a restless night, my mind wouldn't stop.

Chapter 37

The next morning I was up early, but knowing that I didn't have to drive to or around Chicago, and that I had all day to make the 6 hour drive to Marengo, Illinois, I took my time getting ready for the day, and after checking out of my room I went to the truck stop and had a good breakfast. It was just what I needed to get the day started. I was on the road by 10 am, and was actually excited to get where I was going.

I only stopped a couple of times, and I was in Marengo earlier than I needed to be. Since it was Friday, we would have all weekend to spend together if we wanted to. If not, I would start the trek back home. I was close enough that I could do it in one day. I found a coffee shop, and whiled away the time there. When it was time to meet Michael I headed out to his house. When I got there he wasn't there yet, so I just sat in my car and waited. I didn't have to wait long. He pulled into the driveway about 10 minutes after I had arrived. Suddenly I had butterflies. I had not had this feeling in a long time. Right then I knew that Michael was going to be someone very important in my life. What that role was I didn't know for sure, but I knew he would be part of my life for a long time.

We got out of our cars and hugged each other. It felt good. I missed having someone to hug, to hug me. We chatted outside for a few minutes, and then headed into the house. He was separated from his wife at the time, and had a baby girl. As it turned out, this was not his weekend to have her, but he showed me lots of pictures of her. She was adorable of course. After that we sat on the couch and had a beer, just chatting, getting to know one another. At one point he put his hand on my arm and I got goose bumps. We were having so much fun together, I thought it couldn't be a bad sign. Michael knew by now what I had been through, not in great detail, but he knew enough to know that I was terrified to ever get involved with anyone again. He was in the same spot as me really.

After his wife left with his baby girl, he was crushed. Right then and there he had no desire to get involved romantically with anyone. That was fine with me.

We decided we would go out for dinner, and then to his favourite spot, the casino. I was not all that familiar with casinos, but I knew how to play the slots and black jack. He played Caribbean Poker, which I had never heard of, and certainly didn't know how to play. So I was content to stand behind him, watching him play, trying to figure out how the game worked. By the time we left I had a general idea, but not enough to play it. He said he would teach me, since it was still early enough in the evening he would do it when we got back to his place. I wouldn't be confident enough after that night to play the game at the casino, but I at least understood the game more.

Since it was Friday night, and still relatively early, we decided to watch a movie. So we were both on the couch, and of course he had to pick a horror movie. I yelped and jumped more than once, and then all of a sudden his arm was around me, he was laughing at how scared I was, but was trying to make me feel safe at the same time. With his arm around me I felt good. To this day I'm not sure who made the first move, but the next thing I knew we weren't watching the movie anymore. We were on the couch kissing. Even though neither of us wanted to be involved with anyone, neither of us were stopping either. We ended up in his bed, making love. Afterwards I was laying there trying to figure out what I was feeling. Apparently he was doing the same. At the same time we both started talking. It wasn't awkward at all, we both had no regrets, and we were both all of a sudden open to having someone in our lives, preferably each other. So there I was, in Illinois, and my heart was leading me down a road that was terrifying. But, I felt good, I felt hopeful, and I liked feeling this way. Knowing that he was feeling the same way made it that much better.

I eventually made it home, after spending a couple of weeks with Michael. By the time I left I was falling in love. I had no idea how to work a long distance relationship, or if it could even work, but I was invested enough to give it a good chance, and Michael was as well. I don't know if he was feeling as strongly as I was at that time, but he felt enough to know he wanted more. So we spent the next three years in a relationship that was very trying at times, because of the distance, but it was also one of the happiest times of my life. Even though we are not together as a couple anymore, he is still a very important friend. He was the man that made me realize I could trust another man. They really weren't all like Tom and James. He was a good one, and I was lucky enough to have him in my life. I truly owe him so much for making me see that I was worth caring about, and that I could love again.

It isn't easy having a long distance relationship. It's a lot of work, but it makes the times together so sweet. We had as many weekends and holidays together that we possibly could over the next three years. Seeing him was fantastic, but having to go our separate ways each time was excruciating for me. I wanted to be with him all the time. Eventually we both realized that as much as we wanted to be together, it just couldn't happen, and we had to end our relationship. I still loved him, and I think he still loved me, but the distance was the problem. In the end, it was a hard decision to make, but it was the best for both of us. I may not have agreed with that at the time, but looking back later I knew it to be true. To this day I still thank him. Without him I would still be broken, and would not know how to love or be loved.

Chapter 38

Soon after returning home from my journey I was able to go back to work fulltime. Physically I was fine, emotionally I was much better. However, it was going to take me a long time to be fine.

My coworkers had only heard the "need to know" details of what had gone on with James. So I tried to explain to them exactly what I had been through, but I guess unless you have lived it you can't completely understand it. In fact, ashamed as I was to admit it, I had previously been one of those women who couldn't understand why a woman would ever stay with an abusive man. I didn't know that most of them felt they had no choice but to stay. The men, or at least the man I had, if he could be called a man, had broken me down on an emotional level so far that I didn't have much self-esteem left. At one point I was starting to believe that I couldn't make it without him, and had the last time I ever saw him not been as violent as it was there was a chance I would still be with him. I was alienated from friends and family, and now I was trying to repair those relationships. It was going to take time and work, some people more than others, but I knew that I would surely find out who my true friends were. That was a small blessing in disguise. I didn't need people that were in my life for the wrong reasons anymore; it was time to rebuild my life, with strong and supportive friends.

Sometimes I was still scared to be alone at night. I knew he would never be back, but a person can't turn off their fears, especially after dark. I would either stay up so late that I would literally be falling asleep at the computer, or watching television. I wasn't getting the sleep I needed, and I was not eating the things I should have been eating. I also picked up a bad habit during this time. I was drinking alcohol far more than I needed to. I found out that if I drank enough I could sleep, and not have the nightmares. At the time I knew what I was doing wasn't healing, it was just digging a deeper hole, but rational thoughts were not the kind of thoughts I had in the dark. I hid my drinking from everyone, Michael included. In the end I believe that much of the blame for our split lays on my shoulders, because I was drinking so heavily.

A co-worker who had become a good friend to me told me one day that she was thinking of moving. She wanted a bigger place, in a better neighbourhood, but she couldn't afford it on her own. She asked me if I wanted to get a place with her. On one hand I thought it might work out well for me. With someone there after dark maybe I could finally get past some of my fears. I knew that the memory of that night would never leave me, but I wanted to be able to claim my life back. He couldn't have it anymore, not one bit. On the other hand, how well did I know her? I knew she was married, and that she told everyone her husband worked construction. According to her he was only home once every couple of months, so he wouldn't really be living there. I am and always have been a believer in people. I take them at face value, so I didn't think any more about her husband. Would I be able to live with someone else? I wasn't sure I could, I liked things my way, and having a roommate would mean living with her habits too. I decided that I would talk to her about it over dinner. Not in the office where we were interrupted by work and couldn't really have any kind of serious conversation. She agreed, and we went out for dinner to talk. Before the dinner I had thought long and hard about the whole situation, and I had decided that if we could find a place we both liked and could afford the rent, I would give it a go. So that was how I started the conversation at dinner, after all the small talk was exhausted. She was happy about it, and wondered where I wanted to look for a place. She said it had to be on a bus route, since she didn't have a car. I was surprised by that, it was something I had just taken for granted, and had never paid attention to how she got to work or got home. We came up with a few areas that both of us would be comfortable in. Unfortunately there was no way to stay in the neighbourhood I was in because it wasn't close to a bus route, and in the back of my mind I was thinking that would present a problem, and I thought she might expect me to drive her around. I wasn't going to be her chauffer, so I told her that as gently as I could. She said she wouldn't expect that of me. One issue resolved. Things might not be so bad.

I could tell she had something on her mind that she wanted to tell me, and after we finished dinner and were relaxing she decided to finally tell me whatever it was.

What I heard coming from her mouth shocked me, and to be honest, scared me a little.

Her husband was not a construction worker. He was not away working. He was in prison. For manslaughter. It had been a drug deal gone bad. He had been sentenced to five years in prison for the manslaughter and two years for the drug charges. I'm sure my jaw hit the floor. That was the last thing I was expecting to hear. I had so many questions, but I couldn't ask any of them because I was so dumbfounded. Manslaughter? Really? I wondered how she expected me to react to that, and I think she knew my reaction wasn't going to be what she wanted. She started to downplay it all. Her husband hadn't meant to kill him, when he shot at him he was aiming for his leg. Really? Either she was a bad liar, or he had incredibly bad aim since the man he killed was shot in the chest. She said that it wasn't really her husband's fault. The other guy had threatened to shoot him. As for the drugs, she and her husband didn't do any drugs; he just sold them for extra money. Now that one I wasn't falling for. I didn't know how long he would be in prison, and I didn't care. I told her right then and there that there was no way I was going to move in with her. I wasn't going to risk my life over drugs. I had never done drugs in my life, and certainly wasn't going to start living that life now. I was furious with her that she hadn't been honest with me before I had made my decision. She didn't understand why I was so upset. She pleaded with me, but I stood my ground. I didn't need to go from living one hell to another. And I wasn't really buying that she and her husband didn't do drugs. But, that was their choice, and my choice was to not be associated with anyone living that lifestyle. I told her as much, and made sure she knew that there would be no friendship anymore. I would be courteous and professional at work, but from that point on I didn't want to know anything about her life, and certainly would not be confiding in her anymore.

I left the restaurant so angry that I had stormed out without paying my bill. I was halfway home and realized what I had done, so I turned around to go back and pay my share. I walked in and she was still sitting in the booth, but with three other people now. The three people she was sitting with had been sitting in the bar the whole time we had been there, and now I was suspicious. I had to know who they were. I walked back to the table and asked her who her friends were. She tried to shrug it off like they had just run into each other just as she was leaving, and she decided to stay and have a drink with friends. I asked her if any of these three lived with her now, because I had heard rumours that she had roommates already. She started to tell me no, when one of the boys, and that's what they were, boys, but at least one of those boys was honest with me and told me they did live together. I just shook my head and walked away to pay my bill. On the way home again I wondered if they were planning to move in as well, and felt like I had dodged a bullet, pun intended.

By the time I got home I had calmed down enough to relax and watch television for a while before bed. I also checked in with Emily, and told her what had happened at dinner. She was relieved to know I wouldn't be moving in with her at all. The next day I went to work, and never spoke a word to her. She kept her head down, and averted her eyes every time I looked in her direction. That was fine with me. I was still angry, and I felt betrayed as well. I really had steered myself away from a bad situation, and I was pleased about that. I was also impressed with the strength I had in the face of that. It was a huge step. I had just proved to myself that I was going to be okay. I may not be the same woman right now, but I was certainly going to be strong, and be the woman I was before I had met James. Life was starting to look up for me.

Chapter 39

Having put the issue of moving and having a roommate behind me, I focused again on my adoption search. I read through over 200 emails, and decided that I needed to find a way to receive fewer of these emails, without missing any important information. That sent me back to all the websites, changing some settings, and of course I read things on almost every site I went to. I had started this Sunday morning while I was having my coffee, and before I realized it, it was dinner time. I made a light dinner and decided to just relax that evening. Tina called me after dinner, and said she needed to get out of her house for a while, so she came over for a visit. It was nice to see her, and a nice way to spend Sunday evening.

Monday was back to work, but with a twist for me. I was starting my training to work on the answering service side of the business. I found I was quite nervous, and the girls assured me that was normal. I was kind of overwhelmed by the time I left work that day, and wondered if I had made a mistake in agreeing to switch my job position. The good thing about it was that I was so tired, not from doing anything physical, but that mental exhaustion I'm sure everyone has felt at one time or another, and I was actually able to sleep that night. When I woke up I didn't remember any nightmares, and that was a first since that night.

Tuesday was a bit better, but there was so much to learn I wasn't sure if I was going to be able to handle the job. I am very shy when it comes to meeting new people, and it felt like I was meeting hundreds of new people all at once. Even though it was a bit better that day, I still went home feeling uneasy about my decision.

I decided I would get online and see if Emily was around that night, just to have a conversation with someone that didn't involve James or work, and hopefully get them off my mind for a while. As soon as I signed in she sent me a message wondering where I had been the last couple of days. I told her about training for the new position, and seeing a friend, and that I just had been too tired to get online.

We talked about my adoption for a while, and she was telling me she had done some searching, and had sent me a few emails. That made me giggle, she had sent over 40 emails in the last week. If that was a few, I hated to think how many would be a lot to her. I ate my dinner at the computer that night, chatting with her for a long while, until I finally said I had to get off the computer and get to bed, I had to start work at 7 a.m. the next day, instead of 8:30 a.m. So I turned my computer off, got ready for bed, and crawled under the covers with my book. I felt very relaxed that night, more than I had in weeks. I realized how nice it was to have a friend who wasn't directly involved in my life, someone that I could really talk to about things. From that point on I knew Emily would be in my life for a long time, and that felt good.

The rest of the week went by quickly. By Thursday I felt much better about the answering service position, and had even taken some calls that day on my own. Up until then I had someone listening in, sitting beside me, and helping me out. Friday I flew solo. I left work at 3 p.m. feeling quite proud of myself. I knew by then that I was going to like it there, and having worked shift work before in my life, I knew that I would be able to adjust to that fairly quickly.

I spent the weekend catching up with Tina and Kim, and cleaning my apartment. I hadn't done much really since I had come home from the hospital, just the surface cleaning really, so that if someone should come over it wasn't a complete mess. Saturday morning when I got up I felt ready to go through the whole place, ridding it of any trace of James. I knew that his clothes were still there, and I didn't know what to do with them. Did I keep them in case he wanted them? Or did I just get rid of them? That thought was in the back of my mind as I went through everything, closets, cupboards, drawers and all. Saturday night I was exhausted, but it felt good. I had gone through everything in the apartment, giving it a good cleaning as I went along, and I had five boxes of James's things in the closet. Now to decide what to do with them. I gave Kim a call Saturday night, and asked her opinion. The first thing out of her mouth was burn it all. That made me laugh. I should have known that was the reaction I would get from her. So I asked her, other than burning it all, what should I do? She said it was completely up to me. I could take it to a thrift store and donate it all, or throw it all away. She thought either was a fair decision, seeing what he had put me through.

I hadn't thought of thrift stores, and I decided that was a good idea. Someone else might as well get some use of all of it, since he wasn't coming back for it. He was still at large, but I wasn't really that worried about him. If he came back, and the police found him, he would be going to jail, possibly prison, for a long time.

I couldn't get the boxes out of there on Sunday, since the stores that were open wouldn't take donations until Monday. That was okay too, I could drop them all off on my way home Monday from work. Once that was done he was out of my life completely. It was a great feeling knowing that. I knew he would be running somewhere, maybe with another woman. I just wished that if he was with someone else I could warn her. I did worry that he would end up killing someone. It wasn't worry for him; it was worry for the poor woman that got involved with him.

After dinner Saturday night I chatted with Emily a bit. I looked forward to talking to her every day now. She was always able to make me smile, and make me rationalize anything negative that was going on. She surprised me that night with her daughter and granddaughter. I was two years older than her daughter, and had only heard about her through Emily up until then. Her daughter's name was Jennifer, and her granddaughter's name was

Holly. Holly was eight years old, and she took a while to type out her messages. That was okay, it was fun chatting with her, and when she was saying goodbye she called me Auntie. I was so touched by that I had tears in my eyes. These people in British Columbia were becoming more important to me than I had realized. Because I had no contact anymore with my family, they were quickly becoming my surrogate family. It felt good. I missed the feeling of family, and talking with them. Emily went to visit with them, and I puttered around the apartment for a while before going to bed early.

Sunday I spent relaxing, going over Emily's emails in more detail. She sure had sent me a lot of information on the Quinn's in this country, and all around the world. I had no clue how she found it all, and I wondered if any of these people really were my family. It was exciting to think that I might find my half-brother, or my mother. I hoped that if and when I did it would be a positive thing in my life.

That was how my weekend ended. Monday I was actually working the afternoon shift, 3 p.m. until 11 p.m. I hadn't done that in many years, so I was looking forward to it. I would have the mornings to myself, which would be different, but hopefully I wouldn't waste them. I hoped that I would get things done before I went to work. Time would tell.

Chapter 40

I enjoyed my life over the next few months. There wasn't really anything too exciting going on, I was just working, catching up with the girls on our regular nights out, and working on my adoption search. Of course I chatted with Emily almost every day as well. If I didn't chat with her I would send her a message just to let her know I was thinking of her.

One day when we were chatting I was mulling over a decision, and asked her opinion. She gave me her opinion, and then at the end of it she just said that's Mom's opinion, you have to decide yourself. I was shocked to see her call herself Mom, but I did feel like she was more of a mother than I had ever had. I felt wanted, and even though I had never met any of them, I felt like I belonged. It was a good feeling.

Life was pretty good for me. I was settled into the routine of working shift work. I was doing well at the answering service, and had been told by my boss that I was already one of his top operators. I was shocked to hear that, and when he told me that he said that I was certainly ready for more responsibility if I wanted it. I had no idea what he was talking about. What kind of responsibilities I wondered? I didn't have to wonder for long. He offered me a position as a shift manager. Because it came out of the blue I asked him what exactly that meant. I would be in charge of the other operators on my shift, which also meant if there were any problems I would be the one held responsible. I would still be working every shift, that wouldn't change. Up until then there weren't any shift managers. We just went in, did our job and everyone was equal. By that time I was also doing the dispatching for two of our towing companies which entailed not only taking their calls, but actually dispatching the drivers after hours and on weekends. I really enjoyed the dispatching because most of the drivers were great to work with, and as we all got to know each other more we had some fun on the radios if there was a slow time. There were also a couple of drivers that lived near our office, so if they were coming by they would ask me if I wanted coffee. It was great, they would come and drop of coffee for us, but I soon realized that it was only when I was doing the dispatching that they would do it. It was kind of awkward in the beginning, knowing that I was a favourite of theirs, but I got over that quickly. They became good friends over time, and I actually spent time with a few of them when we weren't working. There was no thought of anything romantic with any of the guys, and at that time I was still in a relationship with Michael. However, they did reinforce my realization that there really were some nice guys out there, guys that I could be friends with, and gradually build up my faith and trust in men again. It actually felt like therapy sometimes, especially the first time I met up with one of them outside of work. I was extremely nervous doing that the first time because I didn't know what he was thinking as far as any kind of relationship, but I knew that I wasn't thinking anywhere beyond friendship. It turned out that he was thinking the same thing. That was a huge relief. He had just gotten out of a relationship that, according to him, had not been good for a long time, but it was comfortable, and he had stayed longer than he should have. So we got together when we could, and it was great having a male friend that didn't expect anything more from me. We included a few more of the drivers over time, and we ended up with five of us that would get together when we could, either all together, but most times only a few of us because they worked shift work as well, and didn't always have the same days off. When we did get together it was a lot of fun.

Being that it was finally summer one of the guys suggested that the next time all of us could get together we should go to his place for a barbecue, and sit around the fire pit afterwards. That made me nervous again, hoping that he wasn't thinking of anything romantic, but I found out I was nervous for no reason. Nothing was different, other than we seemed to have a lot more fun. We didn't have to watch how loud we got, whereas at a bar we had to keep it down a bit. We got to listen to the music we wanted to as well. So that was how my summer was spent. Getting together with all of my friends for barbecues, working on my adoption search, and getting to know Emily and her family more and more.

Life was great. I hoped it would stay that way for a long, long time. I was happy. I hadn't been this happy for a few years, and it was wonderful. I got to know a lot more about myself over that first year alone. The best part was that I actually liked me. I came to the realization that even though my last two relationships had ended in a lot of heartache for me, they were part of who I was now. As Emily said many times, everything happens for a reason. And she was right.

Towards the end of the summer, into the beginning of the fall, I had found a chat room online that I was spending a lot of my spare time in. There were people from all over the world, and since I worked shift work, I was able to chat with most, if not all, of the people that frequented the room. I soon found out what all the buzz was about, and finally how people felt about meeting others online. I was becoming quite close with a few people, a couple of men and more than a few women. To this day I am still in contact with many of them, having great friendships with all of them.

Chapter 41

By the time the holiday season came that year I was loving my life. I had all I needed, a job, a roof over my head, and best of all, great friends. Over the holidays there were many invitations extended to me to spend Christmas with people. They didn't want me to be alone. I had so many people that wanted a piece of me on Christmas Day that in the end I decided I was going to have a dinner at my place. I would make a turkey dinner with all the trimmings, and we would call it our Christmas Day. That way they all had a piece of me on Christmas Day.

I had never done a dinner that size on my own. I was doing all kinds of things that I had never done alone, and it was all a learning process for me. The dinner was a huge success; there were some couples there, and some single people. It was great. I was tired by the time the day was over, but it was the kind of tired feeling I would welcome anytime. I had decided that I would make the dinner for 1 p.m. because some people had other parties that same night, so I was up very early to get it all done before people started arriving. The first knock on the door was just before 11 a.m., and it was Tina and Kim. They had decided between themselves that they were coming together and a little earlier than anyone else since I had told people to come any time after noon. Their families would still be there, just later. It was great to have time with the two of them alone. Just like old times. We all worked away in the kitchen getting everything on cooking and ready to go for the dinner. Of course we had some wine while we were doing it, and before anyone else arrived we had polished off a big bottle. The three of us were a little giggly by the time others started to arrive, but it just set the mood for the day. Leave your troubles at the door was the theme of the day. There were gifts for everyone to open, and I was so impressed by my decorating. I wasn't that type of woman. I still had the farm girl in me, and I wasn't much into decorating. But I did buy a full size tree, put it up, and decorated it by myself. To some people that sounded so sad, but I set them straight. I was anything but sad. I was grateful to be alive. The year had been extremely hard on me to begin with, but once the rough parts were over I came out of it alive and well. Seeing my friends all in my home, enjoying good food and great company, I was extremely blessed. There was only one thing missing. Michael.

I was proud of myself as well, for coming out of everything in a positive frame of mind. I could easily have been bitter, but I had decided months before that I would not waste the energy on being bitter. I wasn't going to let men drag me down.

I had offered to work the Christmas shifts at work since I had had my big dinner already, and that way more people with families were able to be home. It was slow at work, so I worked twelve hour shifts on Christmas and Boxing Day. New Years Eve and New Years Day were the same. I didn't mind working them, since I had no plans. So I brought in the New Year at work. Maybe not fun for some people, but, I figured that I would be happier at work than at home alone. I was right. Being at work kept me busy, and didn't give me a chance to miss my loved ones, or just be sad in general.

Chapter 42

Early in the New Year Emily, out of nowhere, said that I should move to British Columbia. I just laughed it off, thinking she was kind of crazy.

My adoption search hadn't really changed much. I was in contact with some people who could possibly be my relatives, but even they weren't sure. Emily was convinced they were cousins, aunts, and uncles. She was also sure that she had the family tree way back into the 1800's. If it was my family it would be exciting confirming that I had all these relatives.

Every once in a while she would mention that I should move to British Columbia. Especially in the winter when I was trudging through foot after foot of snow with no end in sight. She would tell me how nice it was there, and brag that she had no snow to deal with. In March or April I actually started toying with the idea of moving. Other than friends, there was nothing holding me where I was. I had moved relatively close to my adoptive family, hoping that there would be some kind of reconciliation, but it hadn't happened by that time. I was sure it never would. But, in British Columbia I would have family again. It was tempting. I wasn't ready at that point to pick up and move across the country, but it was something I would consider more and more over the coming months.

Chapter 43

Before I could consider moving I had to try to reconcile one more time with my adoptive mother. It wasn't a decision that came lightly to me. I spent many weeks, if not months, trying to figure the best way to approach her. I wrote a letter to her first, just touching base, letting her know that my life was good now. I never heard back from her. It was almost fall by the time I got up the nerve to phone her. I sat down one Sunday afternoon, feeling incredibly anxious, and bit the bullet.

I dialed the number from heart. It was the same phone number I had had when growing up. I think most people remember their first phone number. It was one of those quirky things. It rang once, and all of a sudden I got a recording. It didn't sound like Dad or Mom, and I realized it was a recording saying that the number had changed. I was in so much shock I didn't even write the number down. I had to call back again to get it. It was a number in the town I had gone to school. They sold the farm? Wow. I had no idea, and I knew that the recordings with a forwarding number message only lasted for three months, so I guess I was lucky to find out at all. I was sad the farm was no longer in the family. Even more, I was angrier that she knew how to contact me, had obviously not told Dad that she knew, and that she didn't care if she ever had contact with me again. If I had to admit it, I was extremely hurt. I didn't understand how a mother could just turn her back on her child, adopted or not. She was an extremely unforgiving woman, and I guess I had known that all along, but there was a small piece of me that wanted to believe she wasn't as cruel as I thought she was.

Finding out about the farm the way I did, I had to decide if I wanted to try to reconcile or not. If I did phone, and Mom answered I knew it wasn't going to go well. I knew we would get into a fight, and she, more than likely, would scream at me and then hang up. I just couldn't bring myself to call that day. I needed to process all this new information. I think that was what finally cemented it for me, I would never have contact with them again, and I had to find a way to reconcile myself with that.

That was not going to be easy; it was almost like a death, except it was my whole family that was wiped out. How could she be so vindictive? I felt like I was nothing, that I didn't matter to anyone, or belong anywhere. It was a hard slump to come out of. I needed some time to think through this one. So I didn't call that weekend, or the next. It was at least a month before I screwed up the courage to do it.

Chapter 44

It was a Sunday afternoon again. I had just come home from work, and I was feeling down. Something had to change, I was sad, and had been since I made the phone call to what I thought was still my childhood home. I had done a lot of crying over that month. I felt like an orphan, and I certainly had a new perspective on life. I was alone. I had friends, but friends cannot take the place of your family all of the time, and vice versa. This was one of those times. Good or bad, they were the only family I had ever known.

As was usual in my life, I had not really talked to anyone about it. I had told Emily and a few other people about finding out about the farm, but had brushed it off as if I was okay with it. Just another bump in the road. Honestly though, I couldn't believe how it had affected me. I had always been one to overcome difficulties in my life without anyone else's help. This time was different.

I couldn't get it out of my head that I had almost lost complete contact with my father. I wondered how close I had come, how much longer that recording would have been on the phone line. I decided to call the number again, to see if it was still on. I did. It wasn't. So I had come within a month or less of losing touch. A matter of days. I was angry again. That had been happening a lot over the last month, and I didn't like it at all. I wanted to be me again. I started to wonder if that would ever happen.

I finally decided that I would talk to Emily about it all. I knew that she would put it all in perspective for me. She always could. So I waited for her to come online, but she didn't that night. I went to bed feeling more confused, more hurt, and still angry. My last thought before going to sleep was that it was a good thing I had the next couple of days off because I was in no frame of mind to listen to other people's troubles, which happened a lot, since we answered for doctors' offices mainly.

Monday morning I slept in a lot later than normal. I had tossed and turned all night, and saw every hour on the clock until about 5 a.m. When I did get up I was still tired, and decided that I was just going to take it easy that day. Maybe even have a nap later.

Overnight I had tried to rationalize all of this. Why was I so upset? I hadn't lost the chance for contact with Dad, and I should be thankful for that. Instead all I could feel was anger towards my mother. Even after deciding I was going to take it easy that day I knew I wasn't going to relax at all until I made the phone call that I was dreading. So I made coffee, had some breakfast, had a shower, cleaned up the apartment, all in an effort to put it off as long as I could. I was kind of waiting for Emily to come online. Maybe if I talked to her beforehand I would be able to tackle this in a different frame of mind. She didn't come online, and all I was doing was thinking about how horrible it was going to be, so I decided I had to do it, Emily or no Emily.

I picked up the phone, and was shocked to realize my hands were shaking. I dialed the number, and heard it ringing. Someone picked up. I was holding my breath, hoping it would be Dad. It wasn't. I decided that I was just going to ask for Dad, so I did, and my mother asked me who I was. Really? She didn't know my voice anymore? Wow.

When I told her it was me, she asked me what I wanted. I said I wanted to talk to Dad and she said he wasn't home. I didn't really believe her, but I didn't want to start a fight, so I asked her how she was doing. It all went downhill from there.

"Why would you care how I am?" she asked. "You haven't cared before this how I was, so I don't think it's any of your business how I am now. And it is not your business how your father is. If you haven't heard this, or haven't understood this, I want nothing to do with you. Your father wants nothing to do with you. No one in this family wants anything to do with you. You are the most selfish, immature person I have ever known, and I certainly didn't raise you to be that way. I am still embarrassed to admit that we willingly took you into our home, and adopted you. Face it, we don't want you, your birth mother won't want you. Not one person with any brains will ever want you."

And then she hung up. Click.

I was so dumbfounded that I hadn't been able to get a word in edgewise. I hadn't started to cry though, probably because of the shock of it all. Now I broke down. I couldn't believe that a mother would say things like that to her child, adopted or not. I cried for hours, and finally cried myself to sleep.

When I woke up it was dark, and quiet. I had no clue how long I had been sleeping, and for one glorious second I forgot what had happened. It didn't last though, I remembered, and the tears threatened to start again. I had to suck it up, and forced myself to not start crying. I didn't know what other emotion to feel, so anger was the first one that came through. It definitely stopped the tears. Now I had to figure out what to do with the anger.

It turned out it was just past 8 p.m., and I realized I was hungry. I got up and made myself a quick dinner, and cleaned up. Sitting on the couch, I couldn't concentrate on anything, not my book, not the television, even though I wanted to. I wanted to block this hurt out for a while. It wasn't going to happen though.

Chapter 45

After trying for an hour or more to get my mind straight, and get myself into a better frame of mind, with no success, I decided that maybe doing some searching online might do it. With any luck Emily would be online too. I knew it was almost 7 p.m. in British Columbia, and that she would just be getting home from her part time job and having dinner. Hopefully when that was over she would be online.

I started to look at some of the adoption sites, but all I could hear was my mother's voice repeating, "Your birth mother won't want you." I couldn't get her voice out of my head, so I shut the browser, hoping if I stopped anything to do with my search that it would stop.

It didn't. In fact, it made me feel worse again as the whole tirade that came from her echoed in my head. This time though, I didn't want to cry, I wasn't as angry as I had been, but what I did feel was determination. Determination to not lose my contact with my father. I decided to sit and write him a letter, hoping that if I got the courage to send it, he would actually get it.

I worked on a letter for the next hour or so, until Emily finally came online. I had finished, really, with the letter to Dad, and I was feeling better emotionally. Not great, but better. I had not mentioned the phone call with Mom at all and I didn't know if he would find out about it or not. That was neither here nor there. What mattered was that I hoped beyond hope that he would get my letter.

I told Emily all about what had happened over the last few days. I had to get honest with myself too; it was what had been happening for years, not just the last month or so.

She was shocked, and couldn't believe a mother would say that to her child. Or that anyone would say that kind of thing to another human being. She was appalled, and said that she did not think she would like my mother much if she was ever to meet her.

I laughed at that. I pictured the two of them in a room together. My mother having her rant while Emily quietly listened. Once she was done her rant, I could picture Emily calmly telling her how she was wrong, and what she thought about the things she had said to me yesterday, and in the past. My mother wouldn't be able to hang up on her, or walk away from her. It was almost worth putting them in the same room together. If only I could. It's good to have daydreams sometimes.

Emily talked me down off the ledge, so to speak, and thought that the letter was a great idea. She hoped that Dad would get it as well, and suggested that I don't put my return address on the envelope. That was a great idea. I would remember to do that.

Then it dawned on me. I didn't know their new address; I only had the phone number. The sadness threatened to creep in again, but I forced it away. I did an online address search, and came up with their new address. I put the letter in an envelope and addressed it. Now I just had to find the courage to mail it.

I talked with Emily for a while longer, and then realized how late it was getting. I was finally feeling tired, so I quickly got ready and into bed. I just hoped that I could sleep.

I couldn't. It was another long night.

Chapter 46

I was very tired when I went back to work on Wednesday, and I was very short with people I noticed. That wasn't good. I had to get past this so that I didn't end up losing my job over it. I needed sleep. But how do I get past it? I hadn't mailed the letter to my Dad yet, maybe that was the key.

After work that day I went straight home and grabbed the letter. I drove to the nearest postal drop box I could find, and walked up with it in my hand. I took a deep breath, and dropped it in. There. It was done. It was out of my hands now and all I could do was wait, and hope that Dad got the letter and replied.

When I got home I was feeling completely restless, so I decided to take a walk. It was May now, and the temperatures were starting to rise. It wasn't shorts weather yet, but it was nice enough to just wear a sweatshirt and no jacket. I walked around the neighbourhood for over an hour, and finally headed home. I was feeling tired from the walk, and hoped this would be my remedy to sleeping.

When I got home I left a note for Emily, made myself some dinner and then crawled into a hot bath. It was early, but I was so tired I was hoping the bath would relax me even more, and let me sleep tonight.

It worked. I woke up the next morning feeling much better, and actually feeling like the weight had been lifted somewhat. I guess knowing that there was nothing more I could do took most of the tension away. I would still wonder if he got the letter, or if he would reply, but there was really nothing I could do about that. It was up to him now.

I got through the day at work, and had apologized to any coworkers I thought I had been short with. They said I hadn't been at all, so whether they were just being nice or if I truly wasn't, I was just glad they all accepted my apology. And I hoped that I hadn't been short with any clients. That could have greater consequences. I never heard anything about it, so I guess I had done my job better than I thought I had. Driving home I felt good, and I was hoping the feeling would last.

Chapter 47

I ensconced myself in my adoption search over the next few weeks. Emily had come up with a lot of information, and she said that Newfoundland was full of Quinn's. If this truly was my birth family I was going to have a lot of new relatives. Surely some of them would want to get to know me I hoped.

I searched through census records, birth records, death records, family trees, every possible avenue I could think of I went down. Neither Emily nor I could come up with any definitive answers. We couldn't find any records of a boy born when my information said he would have been. I cast the web on the dates of birth wider, and still nothing. I was feeling like it might never happen, but Emily wouldn't let me believe that. She knew that one day we would stumble across the information that would take us right to my family.

The search continued over the next six months, with nothing really getting us closer. There was a possible cousin that Emily was in contact with, but he knew nothing of me, and asked his family if they knew anything. They didn't. As I had suspected she had kept me a secret from everyone. They assured her that if they were able to find out anything more they would let us know. Being such a big family it was hard to keep track of everything everyone did they said.

I continued to search, but certainly not to the extent that Emily did. She said she enjoyed it all, and wanted to do it. I was like a daughter to her now, and she was determined to see me happy. Knowing that Emily wanted me to be part of her family sure helped keep me going. I hadn't heard from my Dad after six months, and I had to assume I wouldn't hear from him. I told myself that I had to put him out of my mind, and try to come to terms with not having my family anymore, or I was going to drive myself crazy. It was the hardest thing I think I ever had to do.

Chapter 48

One day about a month before Christmas that year I was home, planning my Christmas dinner for that year. I wanted to do the same as I had done the year before, have everyone over again for dinner, and have our Christmas dinner early.

I was sitting at the kitchen table, making notes of what I had to do, and the phone rang. I picked it up without looking at the caller id.

"Emma?"

Oh my gosh! It was my Dad! I tried not to cry, but I was so excited to hear from him that I wasn't in control of my emotions at all. We had a great conversation, talking about anything and everything like we always had. It was like no time had passed since we had talked last. He did mention during the conversation that Mom wasn't home, and a light bulb went on. He was only going to be able to call when she was gone and he was home alone. That angered me, but, I was too overjoyed to let it get to me. At least I had a little bit of my Dad. It made me sure that he still cared. If he didn't, why would he make the effort to call me?

It didn't matter. None of it mattered. I was over the moon that I would still have contact with him. He did say he got my letter, so I knew that I could at least write to him when I was missing him. All of a sudden I didn't feel so alone.

When I hung up I let out a yell. I was so happy I didn't know what to do. I wanted to remember every word he had said, and just keep these feelings going as long as I could.

The rest of the day I couldn't tell you what I did. All I could think of was my Dad. I know I told Emily that he had called, and she was very happy for me. She knew how much Dad meant to me, and she had always had faith that I would hear from him.

While I was chatting with her she mentioned again that I should move to British Columbia. She really thought I would be happier there, and I would have her at the very least. I wouldn't be alone in a big city like I was now. She had a good argument. And then she came in for her coup de gras. She said that since my Dad had now contacted me, I knew I could get a letter to him. Did it really matter where that letter was mailed from? She said no, it didn't, and that being a two hour drive from him might be harder on me than being across the country. If I was in British Columbia I couldn't just take a drive by their house on a Sunday, and torture myself knowing that I could never go in.

I had to admit, she was starting to win me over with the idea. I didn't let on to her at that time though. I had to think it all through, and make sure I had made up my mind, one way or the other. Right then British Columbia was winning me over because Emily kept telling me there was no snow there, in fact it was beautiful weather. I was waist high in snow that year. It had been one of the hardest winters in a long time, and it was only December. I couldn't imagine how the rest of the winter was going to turn out.

I continued to plan my Christmas dinner, and kept thinking seriously about moving. Some days just having to fight through the snow and freezing rain I wanted to be there, not here. But I couldn't just move because the weather was nicer there. I knew that once I moved there was a very good chance I would never see my Dad again. He wasn't a young man, and that worried me. But, at the same time, I couldn't see him now, and I didn't know if anyone would ever call me if something bad happened to Dad, so it didn't seem to make much difference where I was.

Chapter 49

I decided to take a couple extra days off before and after my Christmas dinner. Beforehand I would need the time to get everything ready, get all the groceries I needed, and get my place ready for company. It was easy enough to get the time off, I just told them I would work Christmas and Boxing Day again that year. My boss was thrilled since it wasn't easy to get people who wanted to work those days. People wanted to be with their families. I wanted to be with my family too, but that wasn't going to happen, so I figured I was better off at work. It had helped take my mind off what they would all be doing last year, and I was sure it would this year as well.

I had also made a big decision. I was ninety nine percent sure that I was moving to British Columbia. I had not told a single person, not even Emily, in case I talked myself out of it. I planned to move in the spring if I was doing it. That would give me lots of time in the New Year to make all the arrangements, and to ship my things out there. I was going to tell all my friends at the dinner, so it had to be extra special for me. I wanted it to go well, but I didn't know how they would react.

I was so nervous the day of the dinner, and Kim and Tina had come over early to help me make the meal. They could tell something was up, something was bothering me. I couldn't help myself. I told them what my plan was, and begged them not to say anything to the others. They at least deserved to hear the news from me first.

Kim and Tina both were in shock when I said it. I really had kept the fact that I was even thinking about moving well hidden it seemed. They both knew about Emily, and that Emily wanted me to move. They never pressed me for my thoughts on it, knowing that if I decided to do anything big I would talk to them first. Of course they were right. Telling them relieved me a lot. It was out there, I had finally said it out loud. It made it real to me. I was committing myself to it.

Their reaction was not what I had ever expected in my wildest dreams. Almost at the same time they both said, "Well, it's about time you decided to go." Jokingly I asked them if they were trying to get rid of me. I knew they weren't, but they had to tease me a little. They said they couldn't wait to get rid of me. We all laughed. Then I asked them why they thought I should go.

Tina spoke first. She said that I would have Emily and her family there. I would have a mom in my life again, and I deserved that. Kim agreed with Tina, and added that it would give everyone the excuse to visit British Columbia. They both said there was this thing called email, and that the bond the three of us shared wasn't going to be broken by distance.

I was thrilled to hear that. Although I wouldn't admit it, I had just made up my mind. I was still going to tell everyone at dinner that I was still considering it and wanted their opinions because I valued each and every one of them.

We girls got back to making the meal and people started to arrive. I put it out of my mind the best that I could until dinner. I am sure they all could tell I was distracted, but I hoped they put it down to the meal, and all the preparations.

Of course with any big dinner, it never seems to be done at the time you say it's going to be. It was ready only thirty minutes later than I had planned, so I thought that was pretty good. I told everyone to grab a seat, the meal was ready. Once they were all sitting I asked them if we could wait just a minute before starting. It made them all curious. I started out by saying that they all knew how much Emily in British Columbia meant to me, and that she had been after me to move out there. The room was silent. I think they knew what was coming next, but they waited for me to say it. I said it. I said I was almost sure that I was moving to British Columbia in the spring, and I wanted their opinions on it. Was I making the right decision?

Someone hooted, and there was a resounding course of yes, of course, and many more positive responses. I was in tears. I was so happy that they would all give me their blessing, and we all toasted to me moving, and to everything each and every one of us was thankful for that year, and then dug in.

The party was a success. It lasted well into the wee hours of the morning, and I sure was glad I didn't have to get up for work the next day. I had it on a Saturday night, so hopefully no one had to get up early the next day. I looked around the apartment after the last guest left, and looked at the mess. I couldn't clean it up then. I was too tired, so I turned out the lights and went to bed. I fell asleep thinking about British Columbia, and all of the opportunity waiting for me there. I was going to go live on an island. I had always wanted to live on an island. Maybe a little farther south than Vancouver Island, but, I was still moving to an island. I slept very well that night.

When I got up the next day it was almost noon. I knew by the way I felt I wasn't going to get much done that day. I think everyone had had a little more to drink than they planned on, and I was feeling it. I was glad that there had been a couple of designated drivers, and the rest had come in taxis. It wasn't worth driving drunk, and I was glad they were all responsible the night before.

I eventually got the place cleaned up and back to normal, and I was exhausted when I was done. I decided just to call it a day, and grabbed my book and headed for bed. I still had another day off the next day, so if there was anything I needed to do it was going to wait until then.

Chapter 50

Christmas came and went that year. I worked a lot over the holidays, and promised myself I would put the extra money away for the big move. Once I had told my friends, I knew that I couldn't change my mind. They were so supportive, and I didn't want to let anyone down.

On Christmas Day I had a call at the answering service. When I answered I heard, "Merry Christmas!" I knew instantly that it was Emily. I was so shocked. The last thing I was expecting was a call from her. I was tearing up, and just said Mom! She did most of the talking, while all I could do was sit there and shake my head. Emily's daughter and granddaughter were there as well, that was an added bonus. It made my day, and I think I was smiling for days over it. That phone call made me completely forget about my family and their Christmas dinner for a while. It was such a great feeling. I had not had that feeling of total happiness in a long while it seemed. I had decided to wait until the New Year to tell Emily my plans, but my resolve was waning when I heard her on the phone. I fought the urge to tell her. I didn't want to take away from her Christmas, and that was why I was waiting to tell her.

Now I couldn't wait for the New Year to get here so that I could tell her. I was moving to British Columbia. At that point nothing else mattered, and I wasn't going to let anything get in the way of my plans.

Chapter 51

I trudged on through the horrible winter we were having, with the thought always in my mind that next year I wouldn't have to do this. That was reason enough to move to British Columbia. I was tired of shoveling snow and cleaning off my car, let alone fighting through the streets after snowfalls. The city wasn't always on top of it, and there were days that even the main roads weren't plowed when I headed to work. But, none of it mattered really, because I was moving to British Columbia. I had decided on moving at the end of March. I didn't realize at the time that it was Easter weekend. I had looked for flights online, and their lower prices that week had determined when I was going.

A week or so after New Year's I was ready to tell Emily. I had thought through the logistics, and had called a few shipping companies for prices already, and decided that I would send everything by mail. I didn't have to take any furniture or dishes, nothing like that. I would be living at Emily's house until I got on my feet out there. I had to find a job first, and then find somewhere to live.

I waited for a time when I knew she was home, and I had decided to call her, not tell her online. So that weekend when I was home and we were chatting I called her. She couldn't figure out what was going on, why I would be chatting with her, and then call her. I told her to clean out that spare bedroom that she had been telling me she would have to do if I moved out there, because I was almost on the way. It took a moment for her to process it. Then it hit her, and she gasped. She was so thrilled, and she didn't want to talk very long because she wanted to tell Jennifer and Holly that I was coming. I didn't even get a chance to tell her when I was planning to move, and I don't think right then she cared. She was just so happy and excited that I was. Details could wait until later.

A while later she came online, and all she said was that she was finally going to have all her kids at home. I was still so grateful to her every time she told me I was family, and I was relieved that she was so excited about it.

I was happy. Truly happy. I wanted to capture this feeling, and make sure it was burned into my mind. When I needed a lift I could just recall how elated I was at that time, and then I could overcome any obstacle. It worked. Until I wrote the letter to my Dad to tell him what I was going to do. I felt like I was letting him down and that I was taking the easy way out. Instead of staying and trying to fight the good fight to be part of the family again, I was moving clear across the country. I just hoped he would understand what I was feeling, and would be happy for me. It was the hardest letter I had ever had to write, but I did it, and waited for either a phone call, or a letter back.

About a month later, towards the middle of February, I got a letter from Dad. He said he was going to miss me, but understood why I had to go. He wanted to see me before I left, but, that was easier said than done. How did he get away from Mom long enough to get together with me? I knew right then and there that I would probably never see my Dad alive again. I almost wanted to back out of the whole thing, but I didn't. I realized that it wasn't going to change whether I was here or there, so ultimately there was really nothing holding me where I was. It was a golden opportunity, and those didn't come along very often. So I continued to make plans, and even started getting some things ready to go.

I was going to sell my car because I knew it wouldn't make the trip across country. Tina said she wanted it, so of course I wouldn't take any money from her. She wanted to pay me. It was a battle of wills then, and she cracked first. If I wouldn't let her pay for it, would I let her pay for my plane ticket? Of course not I told her, and that was the end of that.

All my furniture. What was I going to do with it all? I decided in the end that the best thing to do was make sure it all went at the same time, so I donated it all to the Salvation Army. They agreed to pick it up after I left, as I would still have the apartment until the end of the month, so that gave them a week to get there. Kim and Tina had keys to the apartment so there would be someone there to meet them. It was all going so seamlessly I was afraid that it was all too good to be true. Nothing in my life had ever been this easy. It remained easy; I would pack boxes and mail them on my days off, and hope that they got there safe. Some things I couldn't let go through the mail, so I would take them with me in my suitcase.

Chapter 52

The next job on my To Do List was to let my bosses know I would be leaving. I wrote a letter of resignation because I figured they would need it for their files. I was also going to ask a few of the people I worked with for a reference, which hopefully would help me land a job quickly in British Columbia.

I had the letter in my car, but for some unknown reason I couldn't get the nerve up to tell them that week. It was nearing the end of January, two months left before I was leaving. I still had time to let them know. I had decided to quit a week before I was moving so that I would have time to wrap up all the loose ends, and say goodbye to my friends. That was not going to be an easy thing to do, but as we already knew, miles can't separate friends. They would truly be in my heart forever. I had many years of good memories, and I knew that, while I would miss them when I moved, I would never forget the times we had been through. There were marriages, there were divorces, there were children, there were losses, but overall, the joyful by far surpassed the sad. Still, I wasn't looking forward to it. No matter how much I prepared myself, I would not be able to say goodbye easily.

Finally, in the first week of February, I found the nerve to tell my bosses that I was leaving. I was ultimately giving them six weeks' notice, instead of the two weeks most people would have. They were more than happy to write me a letter of reference, as were some of the people I worked with. I had made a few friends there, but I knew they weren't the lifelong type of friends. Sure, there would be a few emails to begin with while I was getting settled. I would still want some kind of connection to my old life, but as time marched on, and I became more settled, the need for those friends would dwindle. After all, we didn't have that much of a history, or the bond I had with Kim and Tina. Kim and Tina would always be in my life. I would never stop wanting that, would I? I hoped I wouldn't.

Resigning from my job made it even more real. I had given notice at my apartment already, but that wasn't something that cemented it. Moving was something I had done before, and would do again. Realizing that I had just committed myself to being unemployed, I decided it was time to get the ticket. I was still watching the dates and fares, and was able to purchase the ticket for the Sunday of Easter weekend.

Purchasing the ticket really threw me for a loop. I was really doing this. All of a sudden I was terrified. I was moving almost three thousand miles away, to live with people I really didn't know. I hoped I knew them, and I was almost positive that they would be the people I had met online, not totally different. Still though, it was a huge risk. I had taken risks before, and even when those risks had turned into bad situations, I was able to overcome them. I could do it again if I had to. I just hoped that I wouldn't have to. I wanted some simplicity in my decisions for once. I think I was entitled to it.

The plan was in action now, so I had to start moving on packing some boxes and shipping them. I didn't know how long they would take to get there, but I wanted them there before me. I decided to pack just a couple of boxes that weekend, and ship them, to get an idea of how many boxes I might need, and how much the shipping costs would be on average.

So I spent that Friday night, and Saturday morning, deciding what I could ship first. What wasn't I going to miss in the next month or so, and if I didn't need it in that month, did I really need it at all? Part way through the first box I decided that this was the perfect time to get rid of a lot of junk, so I now had two empty boxes in front of me. One box to be shipped. One box to be donated along with the furniture. That was not as easy as it might sound. The memories that came with certain objects made it hard to part with things that I really didn't have to have, and would just cost more money to ship. I needed a glass of wine.

I called Kim and Tina to see if they wanted to come over for some wine. They both jumped at the idea. Their husbands were great guys, and both said go, since we didn't have that many more weekends left before I moved. I was excited to see them, but I was hoping to put off the packing. I knew I shouldn't, but I just wasn't motivated that night I suppose.

When the girls got to my place they came with more wine in hand. This could be a long night. But that's okay; none of us had plans for the next day. So we started on the first bottle, and sat chatting.

The more wine we had, the easier it was to go through my things. We managed to get through all of the things that I knew would be hard for me to decide. The knick knacks, the mementos, all the things that people save, but have no reason why. It was great to get it done, even though it was a bit of a shock on Sunday morning. We had all camped out that night, and none of us were feeling up to much the next day. Too much wine, but a lot of fun. And there were two big piles in my living room. I just had to figure out which one I was keeping, and which one I was donating. We started going through one of the piles, and laughed as we realized it was the donations pile, remembering some of the fun we had had the night before.

One job done. Now I had to pack up a couple of boxes, and get them to the Post Office. By then the Post Office had outlets in stores like 7-11, and drugstores. That was handy since the regular offices weren't open on Sunday. So I packed the boxes while we chatted, and by noon we were all starting to feel a little better. We were hungry, that's for sure. So we went out for a quick brunch.

Afterwards they headed off to their families, and I went to mail the boxes. It had been a great weekend.

Everything made it to British Columbia, and Emily was thrilled to pick up the first box. It solidified it all for her. She jokingly said she would hold all my boxes hostage if I tried to change my mind. I reassured her that that would never happen. I had made the decision, and I stuck by the decisions I made, good or bad. Nothing and no one could change that.

The rest of the day was quiet, and I spent part of it packing up the kitchen. It was all being donated, but there were a few coffee mugs and dishes that I really wanted to keep, so they were set aside to be mailed. By the end of the weekend I was very satisfied about the progress I had made. I wondered if I was going to need the whole week off before I left, but in the end I decided I would need it. Even just to relax a little, since I didn't have a clue what my life was about to become. Living in someone else's house was going to be strange, it had been a long time since I had lived at home, or had roommates. I was a little apprehensive I had to admit.

By the second week in March I was ready to go. It was my last week of work, then some time off, then the big move. It was coming so fast, but I was excited about it. I talked to Emily everyday online, and she couldn't wait for me to get there. She was just so excited that she would have me there, and could be the mother I never had. To be honest, I was looking forward to that, looking forward to some mothering, something I had never had enough of to be used to.

My last day at work was a Thursday. I was working the 7 a.m. to 3 p.m. shift, and had plans to go out with a few coworkers for a few drinks that night. If I had been paying attention to the activity in the office after lunch that day, I would not have been so caught off guard when one of my bosses asked me to follow him. I walked into the break room and there was cake, and a going away party. I was moved to tears. I had not expected anything like that. It was nice to know I really did have friends there. Of course, that didn't stop me pretending I was mad at them for not telling me. Everyone saw right through me. Before I knew it the day was over. It was time to pack up for the last time, and move on to my new life. The sadness I suddenly felt was a shock to me. I knew I would be sad to go, but thought I would still be happy about it because of the decision I had made to move. Truth be told, I was terrified to leave my comfort zone, and this was a huge leap of faith I was taking. A few of us still met up for drinks, and by the time I got there I was back to feeling positive about the move. We had a couple drinks, and all of us left the bar to get on with our respective lives. There were some teary goodbyes in the parking lot, and lots of promises to stay in touch. I hoped we would.

Chapter 54

The last week I was in Ontario passed in a blur. I thought I was going to have too much time on my hands, but that turned out to be far from the truth. There were visits with people, the last of the packing and cleaning to do, the last minute things that people would do before going on a trip. The difference was that I wasn't coming back. I tried not to think about it too much that week because the more I thought about it the more nervous I became.

I was leaving that Sunday, so Friday night was reserved for my closest friends. Tina and Kim and their families, Tonya and Elliot, and a few others. I didn't want a going away party; I just wanted to have fun like we always did. That request fell on deaf ears of course. We all met up at Tina's place, and there was definitely a party planned. Cake, decorations, lots of drinks, and tears flowing. Stories were told all night long, funny stories, sad stories, maddening stories, but most of all, embarrassing stories about me. All in good fun of course. Looking back, I am glad they didn't listen to me. The party was the perfect send off. I knew I was making the right choice, and I knew that I had the blessings of the people that mattered the most in my life. Those are true friends, the ones that can be happy for you even though their hearts are breaking. It was the perfect night, and would give me as many memories as I would need after the move, when I wasn't feeling so sure of things.

Sunday morning came too fast. When I got up I didn't feel ready. I was terrified. I calmed myself enough to think rationally. I told myself that if worst came to worst I had saved myself many times before. If I had to do it again, I would find the strength and conviction I would need. Thankfully I would never have to put that theory to the test.

Kim and Tina were taking me to the airport. We packed my bags up, and got in the car to go. Everyone was quiet, lost in their own thoughts. When we got to the airport we couldn't talk enough. We held onto each other for dear life, and none of us were willing to be the first to let go. But I had to make the break. I started walking towards the waiting area, knowing that once I hit the security gate, I would have to cross it alone. Passengers only in that area. I understand the reasoning, but, it didn't make it any easier for any of us. Once I was through the security checkpoint I turned around to see Kim and Tina one last time. They were both trying to smile through their tears, as was I. I waved, and smiled and mouthed I love you to them, and then turned around to walk away. I had to make myself put one foot in front of the other, and not look back. I took a deep breath, and walked to the coffee shop. I needed a magazine, some fluff, to take my mind off the fact that I was missing them already. I would never be able to concentrate on a book. I wasn't sure I could read through my tears either, but I bought a magazine and some water, and waited for my flight to be called.

My flight was called, and I suddenly felt butterflies in my stomach. I walked over and handed my boarding pass to the flight attendant at the door. Here I go, I thought. There's no turning back now. British Columbia here I come, ready or not. I walked down that long boarding ramp to the plane, found my seat, and tried to hold back the tears. Deep breaths I kept telling myself. Breathing and trying to read my magazine allowed me to finally stop crying. One more deep breath, and I was ready to go. Let's get this show on the road, get this plane in the air. Goodbye snow was my last thought as we started to taxi down the runway, and I laughed to myself, realizing I was dressed for winter in Ontario. I wondered what the weather was like that Sunday in British Columbia.

Chapter 55

I had a layover in Calgary on the way. It was only an hour, so by the time I got off the plane, and wandered around looking out the windows at Calgary, it was time to board again. The final leg of my trip. A long time in the offing, but finally here. The bonus was that I had never been to Calgary before, so it was nice to see the little bit of it that I did. If only I knew how I would look back just a couple of years later and laugh about being in Calgary on my way to British Columbia. On my way to finding my birth family.

Flying over the mountains was incredible. I had never been to the mountains before, and it was just a beautiful sight to behold. The flight into Victoria was only an hour from Calgary. I spent most of that time just staring out the window at things I had never seen before. When I caught my first view of the ocean I was breathless. Finally, I was going to live near the ocean. I didn't know why I felt the draw to the water, but I always had, and if I could get to water when I was upset, or sad, or feeling any kind of negative feelings, I was instantly calmed. I couldn't say how many problems over the years had been solved by the waterside. Inland lakes, manmade lakes, rivers, it didn't matter what type it was, as long as it was running water. I instantly knew that everything was going to be okay. Now to meet my new family. I had more butterflies, but it was a feeling of excitement, not nervousness.

When I got off the plane I looked around, trying to get the lay of the land. I followed the crowd, heading for the parking lots, and baggage claim. I instantly knew Emily and Jennifer and Holly. With them was one of the tallest men I had ever seen. He was the youngest of the three brothers, Mark. Mark was a foot taller than me at 6 feet 5 inches. He towered over Emily and Holly. Jennifer was taller than me, but not as tall as Mark. The scary thing was that Mark, while being the youngest boy, was also the shortest boy. Randy, the next oldest brother, was 6 feet 8 inches, and Gary, the oldest child, was 7 feet 1 inch. I was going to get stepped on! They were so tall I was afraid they wouldn't see me below them.

We all hugged, and introduced ourselves, then headed to the baggage claim to grab my things. It turned out it was a two hour drive to Nanaimo, so I was going to get to see some of the island. My new home, on an island. How lucky was I? I felt like I was living in a dream. We got to Emily's house, my home now as well, and I was exhausted. I had been travelling since early in the morning, and it was now mid-afternoon in British Columbia. It was three hours later in Ontario, and my body was telling me it was ready to relax. I put my bags in my room, and we all sat around the dining room table talking over a cup of tea. It felt like I was right where I belonged. I was home, and I was happy. This was meant to be.

Chapter 56

Before retiring for the evening, after a long visit, and a great home cooked dinner, I sent out a few emails to let people know I landed safely, and I was comfortable with where I was. The notes were short as I was tired, and my head was so full of all the new information and surroundings I was in.

After dinner Emily brought out some of the paperwork she had on my adoption search. I couldn't believe how much she had, and was more shocked to learn that what I was seeing was not even half of it. She had two big 3-ring binders full of information, plus a lot of loose sheets in piles. It was going to take me forever to get through it all. We looked through a lot of it together at the dining room table, and seeing how the families connected, I was beginning to be more hopeful of finding my birth family among those papers. Emily hadn't been kidding when she said she probably knew more about the Quinn's than the Quinn's did themselves. The family tree was quickly turning into a forest.

The first two weeks I was there were spent acclimating myself to British Columbia. All the new people, the new town, the new home. The weather, I didn't even know where to start when I was talking about the weather. There was no snow at all, and spring flowers were in bloom. It was beautiful. I knew I was going to be very content here. There was no doubt in my mind.

After three weeks I thought I should start looking for a job. Emily thought it was still too early for me to look. She wanted me to be more settled. So I held off for another couple of weeks, checking the newspapers and online job sites in the meantime. I had my resume and references all ready to go, and was starting to get anxious about looking for work. I had found an answering service in the phone book, and decided that was going to be my first stop. The turnaround rate at answering services was high, so I thought there was a good chance I could get a job there, and then continue to look for another job, a job I thought I would want more than that.

I spent a week driving around, dropping off resumes, and applying for those jobs online that I thought I might like. In total, when the week was done, I had put out over 40 resumes, and I felt sure that someone would call me in for an interview at the very least. About the middle of the next week I got a call from the answering service to go in for an interview. I was hopeful that I had found a job. I went for the interview, and was told that I would get a call as soon as they had an opening. That was a little disappointing, but I didn't really have time to dwell on it. I got a call the following week that they wanted me to start after Victoria Day weekend. So in May I started a new job. It felt good to be working again, and I was able to pay Emily some money for room and board.

The next step would be to find a place to live. When I first got to Nanaimo, in that first couple of weeks while Jennifer and Holly had been showing me around I had seen a high rise apartment right across the street from the waterfront park downtown. Jokingly I said that that was where I would be living. A few months later it would turn out to be true. I would move into a bachelor apartment in that very building, but not on the water side. I would be looking at the mountain. That was fine with me because all I had to do was walk across the street and I was at the ocean. It was perfect. So within a few months of arriving in British Columbia I was finding my spot in life there. I had a job, I had a home, and I was starting to make some friends. It was time to get back to the search.

Chapter 57

Emily had continued to work on my adoption search tirelessly. The stacks of papers were growing, but still nothing definitive. I did what I could to help her search, but found sometimes I was too close to the situation, and got lost in the emotions of it. I was ready to find my family. The waiting seemed like torture sometimes. I was so grateful to Emily and her family for making me feel so welcome, so I certainly didn't feel lonely. But they still weren't my blood relatives. My birthday and Christmas were coming, signaling another year of searching with no end in sight.

My birthday had always been the worst day of the year for me. A lot of adoptees say it's the holidays that are the worst, but not for me. Everyone had the holidays, but my birthday was the one day that only she and I shared. I wondered if she thought about me, if she wondered where I was, how I had turned out. I thought about her all day long, every year. I wondered if I had ever passed her in the street, and if I had, did she recognize me. It was harder each year to realize that she was still out there somewhere, but as far as I could tell, she wasn't looking for me. My feelings were no different than millions of other adoptees, but they were mine, and something I had to overcome every year. It was unfortunate that my birthday was so close to Christmas, as it always seemed to put a damper on my holidays. Maybe this year would be different having family to spend it with.

I was scheduled to work Christmas Day, which was okay, and I was getting together with the family on Christmas Eve. Emily had just moved into a new place herself, as the house she had been living in was sold. Even still, she had many beautiful decorations up, and the meal was excellent. After dinner while we were having tea she handed me an envelope. I opened it up, and I didn't understand. It was papers from a search agency in Texas, and they were going to be searching for my birth mother and brother. I was dumbfounded. I couldn't believe that she would do that for me. It was above and beyond anything she needed to do, and I was so grateful to her. I couldn't thank her enough. There were some papers to send in yet, as I had to sign some, and she didn't want to give it to me until Christmas. As soon as we could, we would go to the notary and have the papers signed and witnessed that we needed to, and get them off to Texas.

In the meantime I read all about the company. They had a stellar reputation, and had a high success rate in finding lost families or adoptees. The one good fact that I could see was that they would not stop searching. There was no time limit on how long the search would last. It would last until my family was found, and not stop one minute before. If it took two years, or five years, it didn't matter. It was exciting.

Emily, of course, continued her search independently. She found people, emailed people, and tried to find a connection to me, but mostly wanted to find someone that could say, yes, they knew about me, and they were my family. She felt she was close so many times, but just couldn't get that concrete evidence to say that she had found them.

The next year of my life was fairly uneventful. I worked, I spent time walking the waterfront, and I spent time with friends and family when I could. I was feeling like I had been there for years, it was such a comfortable feeling. My office was a five minute walk from my apartment building and after work most days I would take the scenic route, and walk the waterfront. It was a great stress reliever, and some days I just sat on a bench, letting the day go before I got home. I could see Gabriola Island off in the distance, and I would wonder if I would get there someday, just to see it. I was loving life. Especially the winters. Two or three inches of snow fell that first year, and lasted for only a day or two. However, that two or three inches of snow almost shut the city down and almost completely exhausted the city's snow budget. I was so amused. Two or three inches of snow in Ontario meant that people might get out their winter boots, certainly not shut cities down, and have people panicking about being able to get out for food. It was nice not having to deal with the snow since I didn't have a car, but at Christmastime it affected me in a way I never saw coming. I missed the snow, and it just didn't feel like Christmas to me. After ten years here I still haven't gotten used to that. I have had one great Christmas since I moved here, one white Christmas, and I felt like I was home. I have to remind myself that it's the people that matter over the holidays, not the snow, or lack thereof. Not an easy thing to convince myself of, but I was used to putting the smile on, and going along with the flow. I had done it so many times in my life, especially around my adoptive family. I wanted my life in British Columbia to create happy holiday memories for me, and it has, even without the snow.

Chapter 58

Christmas Eve in 2004 was much the same as the first year I had been in British Columbia. I spent it with Emily and the family that could make it that night. As usual it was a great meal, with even better company.

The strangest thing was that Emily, for reasons that made no sense to me at the time, had her email open, and the sound turned up as loud as it would go. I had no clue what she was waiting for, but every time we heard the sound, either Jennifer or Emily would run to the computer to see what had just come in. We continued on with dinner and the festivities, and I put it out of my mind. If it was any of my business they would tell me all about it. If I had only known I had the surprise of my life coming.

Towards the end of the meal I heard Emily's computer again. Jennifer got up to see what it was, and came back out and whispered something to Emily. Then they both disappeared. I sat there visiting, wondering what the big secret was. Jennifer came out smiling so big, but she wouldn't tell me what was going on. Then Emily came back into the kitchen holding a sheet of paper. I expected to see an email that she had been waiting all night for but she told me to come back to the bedroom where her computer was for a minute, she had something to show me.

I sat down in front of the computer, and I saw a picture on the screen, but didn't pay much attention to it. I assumed it was someone in her family that had sent a picture. Emily handed me the sheet of paper, and to my surprise it was a poem that she had written for me, telling me how she wished she could make my dreams come true.

If I Could

If I could give you rainbows to brighten your day, I would.
If I could give you sunshine, to take away the rain, I would.
If I could wave a magic wand and make the world seem right, I would.
I can't, but I would if I could.
Your yesterdays have passed by,
Your tomorrows yet to come.
And with each passing day your dreams have yet to come.
If I could make it easier, I would if I could.
If I could bring smiles and laughter back to you, I would if I could.
Life holds no guarantees of what it might have been
If I could make it easier, I would if I could.
You are an angel, my "daughter" sent from somewhere above.
You joined our family, and brought lots of love.
If I could grant you one great wish, I would if I could.
So my dear daughter Emma, as Christmas draws near,
A special gift I am holding right here.
Open it gently, cherish it do,
Because this gift holds love, do not fear.
As the sun's rays brightly shine on your life today,
Remember this moment, remember past fears,
For in a moment the phone is going to ring,
And the message it brings,
Hello Sister, where have you been?
Merry Christmas my daughter.
I love you so.
Mom

Instantly I was in tears. I knew how much time she spent searching. Hours upon hours, any chance she had. She was invested in this search as much as I was; in fact, sometimes it seemed like more for her. I had expressed to her more than once that I wished I could do more searching, but I was working a lot of overtime, and when I could search I found it too emotionally draining sometimes. Of course she always told me that I did more than enough, and how much she enjoyed doing it. But still, it was hard for me to accept that someone wanted to do so much to help me out. It was not a feeling I had had very often in my life.

After reading the beautiful poem, and hugging her tight, she told me to look at the computer screen. To really look at it. I was looking at a picture of a man and woman, around my age, but I had no idea who they were. I was curious now though, since they seemed to be making such a big deal about it. Emily asked me if he looked familiar, and I quickly answered no. I asked her who it was. Jennifer started to laugh, as did Emily.

"That is your brother and his wife," Emily said.

I was speechless. Completely stunned. My brother? The brother we had been searching for? I just stared at him. Emily and Jennifer kept saying how much we looked alike. I didn't see it at the time, but I was so shocked to be looking at a blood relative of mine. Finally. Emily had found my family. My older brother. My very first link to my roots.

I couldn't speak. I just sat there and cried for what seemed like hours. I had questions, but I couldn't speak. I couldn't put a coherent thought together.

Emily told me his name was Charles, and his wife's name was Becky. His last name was not Quinn though, and that had been the piece of the puzzle that had been missing for so long. They lived in Calgary. My birth mother had eventually married, and her husband had adopted Charles. So his last name was Murphy, not Quinn. Emily had spent all of the previous night, parts of Christmas Eve day, and finally Christmas Eve itself, confirming with Becky that I was indeed Charles's sister. Becky then had to tell Charles that I existed, and I wanted to know him. Apparently, as I had figured all along, no one knew about me. When my mother had left Newfoundland she had left my brother there with his grandparents. She had me before she moved back home, so no one had any clue about her being pregnant while she was in Ontario.

I couldn't take my eyes off him. At thirty-eight years old I finally had my brother. My mind was just a jumble. I needed time to process this, and to figure out where I wanted to go from there. Of course I wanted to jump on a plane right then, but that wasn't going to happen, no matter how much I wanted it. I did, however, want to get to know him. I wanted to know about my family. But first of all I had to go home, and let it all sink in.

Christmas Day I was still on cloud nine, and would tell anyone that was willing to listen that I got a brother for Christmas. I had a computer printout of the picture of him and his wife, and I was showing anyone and everyone. When I got home that day I was emailing it to everyone I knew, and phoning some that didn't have email. I was so excited. I didn't care if I never found any more family, I had my brother, and I had an email from him saying that he wanted to get to know me. I was over the moon, and that feeling would last for a long time to come.

Charles and I chatted online over the holiday season, and when New Year's Eve rolled around I couldn't let the year go out without at least talking to him on the phone. I picked up the phone, and felt the butterflies starting in my stomach. I was so excited, and so nervous, all at the same time. I had been chatting with him online earlier, but as the phone rang two, then three times, I thought maybe they had gone out. Just as I was trying to decide if I should leave a message I heard Becky's voice for the first time. She and I talked for a few minutes, and then she put Charles on the phone. It was a dream come true to hear his voice. We talked as if we had grown up together, like brother and sister, and it felt wonderful. We talked for close to an hour, and when I got off the phone I wondered why I had been nervous at all. It was such a feeling of elation; I didn't want to ever lose that feeling.

While we were talking, Charles said he had to tell me something before we went any further. I braced myself for bad news. I was imagining him saying that he didn't want any more contact, and I was quickly losing the happy feeling. Boy was I wrong. He told me that I have another sibling. I have a sister. She lives in Florida, and she is three years younger than me. She had been put up for adoption as well. Her name was Ella, and she had two children. Just when I thought it couldn't get any better, it did. She had found Charles two years before I did, and they had met in Las Vegas. Becky emailed me pictures of her, and of course I felt an instant love for her. I had a baby sister. She knew about me, and couldn't wait to hear from me, so I emailed her before I went to bed that night.

During our conversation Charles kept telling me I sounded just like our mother, and I looked just like her as well. When I laughed he said he could swear he was talking to our mother. I also found out that I had two more sisters. Charles had been raised with them, and their father was the one that had adopted Charles. I was dumfounded. Just a few days ago I felt like an orphan, and now I had four siblings. It is funny how quickly life can change. This was a great change. I felt like I belonged somewhere now. At least in Charles' and Ella's lives. Right then that was more than enough.

Chapter 59

Early in the New Year Charles and I were comfortable enough with each other to know that we wanted to meet. The sooner the better. So we started to make arrangements.

It turned out that we would be meeting on March 17, 2005. I would fly to Calgary for the weekend. I couldn't contain my excitement, and that day couldn't come fast enough. We were all excited to meet, and I just knew it was going to be great.

Jennifer drove me to the airport the morning of March 17th. Again it was just a short flight, over the mountains and there was Calgary spread out below me. The butterflies started as the plane was touching down. I couldn't wait to get off the plane and find my brother.

When I got off the plane I was looking around, trying to find them. I knew I had to find the escalator to go down, and they were going to meet me there. As soon as I got on the escalator and looked down I could see them. They hadn't spotted me yet, and I could see their mouths drop open when they did. That made me a little nervous, but I tried to put it out of my mind. I swear it was the slowest moving escalator I had ever been on, and of course there was a crowd in front of me, so I couldn't walk down it any faster. As soon as I got to the bottom I rushed over and hugged Charles. We held onto each other as long as possible, then stepped back and had a good look at each other. I hugged Becky, and we headed off to the baggage claim. We couldn't stop talking, and looking at each other. I think we were both in a little bit of shock. The day had finally come.

We headed to their house, and then sat around the table and visited for a couple hours. We had a few drinks, and then decided we should go get some dinner. While we were talking, and they were showing me pictures of the family, they both kept saying that I was the spitting image of our mother. I talked like her, and when I laughed Charles laughed too. He said it was just like Mom.

At dinner as I sat across from him at the restaurant he said he had the strangest feeling that he was having beers with Mom. It was a little surreal to both of us. Finally I looked like someone. I was on cloud nine again.

When I saw pictures of my Mom I saw why they were saying all night that I was a younger version of Mom. I felt like I was getting a glimpse of myself in twenty years. She is a beautiful woman, and of all five kids I am the one that really looks like her. Charles didn't think it was possible to look so much like her, but here I was, living proof.

The weekend was over far too soon. I wasn't ready to go home yet, but I had to. We were definitely family now. I wasn't letting that go. It was so wonderful to be able to look in a mirror now and see my mother's face reflected back at me. Finally I knew who I looked like, and sounded like as well. I hoped one day to meet her, but right then I extremely blessed having met Charles and Becky. If only Ella could have been there too, that would have made it that much more special. I hoped one day soon to meet her and her children as well. I had been in email contact with her, and she was as shocked to find out I existed as I was to find out about her. She had grown up an only child, so she loved that she now had a brother and sisters. She had missed out on growing up with siblings, but was glad she had us now.

I went home to Nanaimo, and back to my usual routine. I was happier than I had ever been, and that hole I had in me all my life was starting to fill up. I couldn't thank Emily enough for all her hard work and she kept telling me that seeing me so happy was thanks enough. She had always known there was a happier person in me, and was happy that she could help her surface. I felt like my life was almost complete now.

Chapter 60

After getting back from Calgary, and having my feet back on the ground, Charles and I talked about our mother. I wanted to know if he thought she would want to know me. As much as it hurt him to say it, he had to tell me no. When our sister, Ella, had tried to contact her a couple of years before the reception was cold. There was minimal contact at first, and that dwindled to nothing. That was a lot for me to take in. I had to reconcile inside myself that I may never know my birth mother, having come this close. At least I had Charles and Ella, and Charles was in contact with our mom, so if anything ever happened to her he would let us both know. It was so nice to have Ella to talk with now. She literally knew exactly what I was going through. We were dealing with the same family members, and neither of us had contact.

A couple months after I came home from Calgary I got a phone call from a woman in Ontario. She worked for the ministry that oversaw adoption information. She was calling to inform me that they had been in touch with my mother. She was willing to give some medical history, which basically turned out to be nothing; it seemed everyone in the family was healthy. That was good news; unfortunately she had to tell me what I already knew. My birth mother didn't want to have contact with me, or know anything about me.

I thought I would be okay with that, since I knew that was likely to be the information that came from the search. But, it sent me into a tailspin. All of a sudden I was depressed and I was flooded with memories of my adoptive mother. Horrible memories. I now had two mothers that rejected me. One of them rejected me twice. It shook me to the core. I didn't know what that said about me. Was I unlovable? Was I such a horrible person that no one would ever want to acknowledge me as theirs?

Chapter 61

I tried so hard to come up with some good memories with my adoptive mother. There were a few, but they were all with the whole family, not just her and I. I didn't, and still don't, remember much of my childhood. I have read that people that didn't have great childhoods quite often blocked out the past. Maybe that was what I was doing. I didn't know. All I knew was that the horrible memories were so crystal clear it felt like I was back in the moment of each and every one of them.

I couldn't stop thinking about my family, my siblings, all older. Two brothers and one sister. My oldest brother is seven years older than me, then there's my sister who is six years older, and my other brother is three years older. We also have a foster brother who has been with us since I was eight. He is only three months younger than me, and I thought maybe he and I would be closer than I was to the rest of my siblings. It didn't turn out that way. We just weren't a close family. At least I didn't think we were. Maybe the others felt that it was a close family. I always kind of felt like an outsider, not just because I wasn't a blood relative to any of them, but because of the way my mother treated me.

When I was a little girl I lived on a farm. My Dad's parents lived right across the road from us on their farm. I loved being there. My Grandma was such a sweet lady. She always had treats, cookies, cake, and milk, as much milk as I wanted. She and I would spend hours having tea parties. I was so happy when I was with her. My Grandpa sat on a bench outside and watched all the farming going on around him. He wasn't able to help anymore, and he missed it. I would sit with him, my feet not touching the ground and swinging back and forth, and we would play games sitting on that bench. Ants in the Pants. My most favourite game ever, hands down. To this day if I see an Ants in the Pants game it almost brings tears to my eyes. We played that game for hours on end. I don't remember a time when he didn't have time for me. Being in their home with them was a safe zone. I will cherish their memories until the day I die.

I would "run away" a lot when I was young. But never farther than Grandma and Grandpa's house. I found out long after I had grown up that Mom would phone them to tell them I was on my way over. In those days no one worried about their kids being out alone, there was not the risk of the crimes against children happening then that happen now. Realistically though, where else was I going to run to? We lived in the country, and there were two farms on our road, Grandpa's and ours. The next neighbours were a mile or more away, and when I was younger I didn't know them. I knew a couple of them had kids my age because I would see them at Sunday school and church. Before I went to school the only friends I had were Grandma and Grandpa, my Dad of course, and Raggedy Ann and Andy. I didn't go anywhere without Raggedy Ann and Andy. That wasn't always easy since they were the same size as me, but I managed somehow.

When I was eight years old my Grandpa died. I don't remember much of it, but I remember seeing him in his casket. That was my first experience with death, at least the death of someone I loved. Sure, living on the farm there were deaths. But those were farm animals. I had some special animals that were all mine, and had something happened to them I would have been very sad. But the death of Grandpa was something totally different. My Dad was so sad, and I couldn't cheer him up. I think that was what made me the saddest. Eventually my Dad cheered up, and that was what made me happy again. Then that same winter we moved over to the other farm, in with Grandma. I was ecstatic. I thought I would have my safe zone in the same house. At first it was great. I spent every second I could with Grandma. I remember her saying to me one time that she wished my Mommy loved me half as much as she did. Being eight years old I didn't understand the implications of that statement. Over the years I learned exactly what she meant.

Before we moved in with Grandma I remember one night I felt my heart skip a beat when I was lying in bed. I was terrified. I ran downstairs and was crying. My Mom told me to get back to bed; there wasn't a single thing wrong with me. I asked her if I was going to go be with Grandpa, and she slapped me in the back of the head and told me not to be so stupid. I was sent back to bed, terrified, and eventually I cried myself to sleep. To this day I still feel my heart skip a beat occasionally, but I've had it all checked out, it's just something my body does. It won't hurt me, and there's no underlying medical cause. I can feel it every time it does it, and it still gives me a scare sometimes, but I guess in the end she was right. I wasn't going to die. But how does a mother treat her child like that? She never treated me like that in front of dad of course; I think he would have protected me more had he known all that went on. I don't fault him for that though. He couldn't fix what he didn't know was broken.

My earliest memory is one of my mother in the living room of the first house we lived in. She was ironing and I was the only one home with her, so the other kids must have been in school. I asked her why she didn't work, and she literally screamed at me. How dare I say she doesn't work? Wasn't she here all day with me, working every minute? Did I think it wasn't work looking after me? I remember crying, and being scared, too scared to run away from her. I should have run. The next thing I knew I was being spanked, and not lightly, and told to go to my bedroom. I shared a bedroom with my sister, and I wasn't allowed to touch anything of hers. When I got sent to my room I knew better than to play with anything, because if she heard the slightest noise she was up those stairs so quick to spank me again. I never once saw her spank anyone else. Maybe I was the only bad kid. I don't believe that though.

I have been highly emotional as long as I can remember. This caused a lot of problems with my mother of course. She called me a cry baby, and told me to grow up. I was eight or nine years old. How fast was I supposed to grow up? The problem was that she was the one causing me the anxiety, and the tears, and the raw emotions, and she didn't see it. It was all me. But being an emotional child did not fit into her picture of the perfect family. Although she would say that she didn't care what the public opinion of her was, you didn't dare cause a blemish on the family, as I found out when I was much older.

It was around this time that I had an extremely scary accident on the farm. I was riding from one farm to the other in the bucket of the tractor, along with some bags of chop for the pigs. My brother was driving the tractor, my Dad was there as well, and a foster brother who was living with us at the time. I was having fun riding there, and the guys were all looking at something in the field, not really paying attention to anything else that was going on around them. Then the bucket tripped as we went over a pothole in the laneway. I hit the ground with the chop bags, screaming because I was so terrified. Of course they couldn't hear me over the tractor engine. To this day I still remember seeing the tractor moving over top of me, and I knew that I was in grave danger. My brother didn't stop the tractor. I could have been killed that day. Suddenly the tractor stopped, but only because one of the chop bags had landed in the track of the tire. That chop bag literally saved my life. My Dad realized what had happened, and he yelled out for me. I couldn't hear him while the tractor was running, and then I heard him yelling when my brother finally shut down the tractor. At the time I only knew it was a kind of yell I had never heard from my Dad before. As I got older and recalled it, I came to realize it came from complete fear, and total adrenaline. He heard me crying and screaming, and tried to get to me. I was literally paralyzed with fear, and he had to make my brother back the tractor up, inch by inch, until he could reach me and pull me out. He hugged me to him to try to calm me down, then pulled away to make sure I was not hurt.

When he had checked me over and was convinced that nothing was broken, crushed or burned he walked the rest of the way home with me because nothing he said could make me get back on that tractor, not even to ride on the back. We held hands all the way, and he tried so hard to take my mind off what had happened by talking about anything else under the sun. I think he was trying to calm himself down as well.

We got home and he dusted me off a little more and took me into the house. He told Mom what had happened, and then had to get back to his work. I was still crying, and quite shaken up, but of course that made no difference to her. I tried so hard to stop crying, just standing there with her staring at me. Once she knew Dad and everyone else were out of earshot she slapped me in the back of the head and told me to stop bawling, or she would give me something to cry about.

Thinking back now, I really believe that I already had enough to cry about without her adding more anguish, but she really thought I had no reason to cry at all. In her mind I wasn't hurt, other than some scrapes and bruises that would show up over the coming days, and she didn't have time for it. I obviously had interrupted her, although I don't know what she had been doing.

Sometimes I wonder if she realized how close I had been to being killed, and maybe she was upset that I hadn't been killed. Later in my life she would admit that she never wanted me. If I died not only would she be rid of me, but she would also get all the sympathy that goes along with it. Sympathy that, in my mind, she was certainly not deserving of. But I didn't die, unfortunately for her, so I was still in her way, and I was just a big baby according to her. I guess there was just no way for me to ever please her.

I still have a colossal fear of anything that gives me a falling sensation. Ferris wheels, roller coasters. Sometimes elevators. Driving down large hills, which can be a problem because I live on an island covered with mountains. It is a sensation that just paralyzes me with fear. I wonder what she would say about that now. Well, I don't really wonder because I know it would be something degrading and plain mean.

My birthday is in November. I had one birthday party all the time I was growing up. She said it was because her house would be full of kids that she couldn't send outside because of the weather. But, my brother was born in December, and he sure had a birthday party every year. I guess the weather was better in December. I sure didn't think so, but again, I wasn't her birth child, so I didn't really count. I would wake up in the morning on my birthday, and no one would acknowledge it was my birthday. When I got downstairs there would be a present on the kitchen table. Sometimes it was wrapped, but more often it wasn't. She wouldn't even take the effort to wrap a present for me; it was usually in a brown paper bag, or sometimes a plastic shopping bag. My Dad would always say happy birthday to me, and try to make me feel special that day. I love him for that. At least he cared enough to do something. There were years that I didn't even get a birthday cake because she was too busy, but, I wasn't in a very celebratory mood to begin with so I pretended it was okay. Of course it just added to the hurt I already felt.

Grandma moved out and into town when I was ten years old. I think all the hustle and bustle of having kids in her house full time again was just too much for her. Maybe it was living with my mom. I wasn't privy to the reasoning; I was just heartbroken that she was leaving me. She didn't drive, so it wasn't like she could pop in to see me, and I knew that mom wasn't going to take me to visit her. From that time on I had less and less contact with her, until one day Dad told me that she was sick and was in the hospital. I was maybe eleven then. She had leukemia, and she passed away quickly. I only got to see her once while she was in the hospital. The next time I saw her she was in her casket. Again, I was young, so I didn't totally understand it. I knew that I would never see her again, and that made me very sad, but I didn't have any concept of forever then. To this day I miss Grandma and Grandpa, and love them deeply. I wish I had had them around longer so that I could have realized my feelings, and had been able to tell them how I felt. I live now with the hope that they are watching me from somewhere, and know how much I love them.

I have always resented my Mom for trying to take away all my good memories of Grandpa and Grandma. She told me more than once that Grandpa was mean, and called my Grandma horrible names. I never saw any of that, and I have since learned that Alzheimer's is definitely something that runs in the family. But why she felt the need to try to turn all my good memories to bad ones I will never know. She was supposed to be the adult in the relationship, but she sure didn't act like it. She never knew that she couldn't tarnish those memories. They were mine, and mine alone. She didn't get to ruin that. I wouldn't let her.

When Grandma moved out all of a sudden my Mom's cruelty towards me ramped up. I was like her slave. I had to work, and not just small chores, age appropriate chores. I had to cook, sometimes for as many as ten people. I had to clean, do laundry, and anything else Mom decided I should do. I had so many chores to do around the house, and homework for school, that I never had time to play anymore. If I did have some spare time, Mom was sure to find something else for me to do.

I didn't have a lot of friends all through school. It was partly because when they would invite me over to their houses I wasn't allowed to go. I had "chores" to do. And very rarely was I ever allowed to have a friend over. However, I remember my brother and sister's friends being around a lot. I remember that because I was the one that had to clean up after them all. I remember crying a lot while doing all this work. Even then I knew it wasn't right, but what could I do about it? I was powerless. Those were not the days when a child could pick up the phone and call a 1-800 number and tell on their parents. You lived with it, and you found a way to deal with it. I felt like I was literally the real life Cinderella, but my Prince Charming never rode in to save me.

It was around that time that more and more foster children started to arrive. Some stayed a few months. Some stayed a few years. They all got bedrooms upstairs. One would share a bedroom with my sister, and another would get what had been my bedroom. I didn't have a bedroom anymore. I slept in the hallway. Everyone had to walk past me to get to their bedrooms, or to the upstairs bathroom, and the floors creaked a lot. I heard every one of them walking past. This was not conducive to my sleep, and went on for at least two or three years. Finally my sister moved out, and I was granted permission to move into a bedroom. Not the one I had to myself before I was put in the hallway. Oh no, I had to share a room now with a foster sister. They were all older than me, so of course they went to bed later than me, and made a lot of noise. I still wasn't getting the sleep I needed, and the lack of sleep made me more emotional. It was a vicious circle, Mom victimized me because I was so emotional, which made me cry more, and around and around we went.

One day I was crying in the shower because someone had made fun of me at school. They had found out I was adopted, and they said I wasn't a real child. Kids sure can be cruel. When I got out of the shower and went upstairs Mom was there. She asked me what I had been bawling about this time, and for some reason I let my guard down, and I told her that the kids at school were being mean to me. She told me to stop my crying, and that she better not hear from my brother that I had been crying at school again.

Sometimes I was just so dumbfounded by her reaction to me. She certainly didn't treat any of the other kids that way.

When I was twelve or thirteen I couldn't help myself, and one day I asked Mom why they had adopted me when they already had three other kids. Had I known the answer I would have never asked. She looked me straight in the eyes and told me she never wanted me, but dad wanted another daughter. She refused to have another child, and adoption became the only option. So dad got his daughter, and Mom got her Cinderella. From that point on my mother and I had basically no relationship. I had to live there, but I didn't have to talk to her. So I didn't. I didn't talk much to anyone in fact. I became very withdrawn and introverted. I had not been an outgoing person before that, but the change in me was huge. I felt worthless, and went about my school work and "chores", and swore to never again voice an opinion to my mother.

At fifteen I met my first boyfriend, my first true love. Mom didn't like him of course. She made him feel very unwelcome in our house, so we did not spend very much time with my family. Dad asked me one time why that was, and I told her how Bill felt when he was around Mom. I tried not to complain to dad too much about mom. It was not going to do either of us any good, and we couldn't fix it, so why bother him with it? Bill's family, on the other hand, was extremely close, and I loved them all. He had one sister, who had been with her long-time boyfriend for many years, and they were engaged at the time. We would spend time at Bill's house, playing cards, watching movies, just being with the family. I was amazed in the beginning at how close they all were. I was a wee bit jealous too. I never told his parents about anything to do with my mom, but I think Bill must have because his mom took me under her wing, and finally I had a mother figure that truly did love me. I felt what a mother's love was supposed to feel like for the first time in my life. Bill was my first love, and I hoped that he and I would be together forever. Of course, I was fifteen at the time. Too young to know any better.

When we first started dating, Bill told me that he had never seen eyes like mine. He said that he had never seen the colour, but also that he felt that they could see through people, right to their very soul. He made me feel so special when he said that. I don't think I had ever been so happy before.

A few months after I started dating Bill my brother in law lost his battle with cancer. He had been so good to me the whole time he was dating my sister, and when they were married. I loved him so much. He always made time for me, no matter what was going on. I was very happy when he was around. When he got sick I was heartbroken, and scared. I didn't want to lose another person that I finally connected with.

He went into remission for a few months, and then was sick again. The second time was much worse, but no one told me how bad. They all knew it was just a matter of time before he passed away, so they were able to say their goodbyes. I never got that chance. My mother had decided that since she couldn't split Bill and I up she was going to send me to my aunt and uncles house that summer to babysit my cousins, and look after the house. I was there when Jerry passed. Another one of my aunts had called early in the afternoon, and she asked if I was home alone. For some reason I knew. I had had a dream about him the night before, and when my aunt called I just knew it had been a sign. I later found out that when I had the dream, it was at the same time that he was passing away. It was like he was coming to say goodbye to me.

When my aunt and uncle told me I was hysterical. I had pretty much known that they were going to tell me he was gone, but to actually hear the words, to make it real, I felt like I had died inside. I didn't know how I was going to say goodbye to him. He was the one bright light in my family, and now I had lost him. My uncle drove me home, and their Chihuahua refused to let me go without her. Blackie had actually been our dog in the beginning, but my brother developed allergies, and the dog had to go. Spending that summer with her was great. I had missed having her around. I had a better connection with pets than with people. I guess because they didn't let me down, or hurt me the way people tended to. When we got to the farm Mom and Dad were just pulling in from picking my sister up from the airport. For the first time I felt close to my sister, and we stood in the driveway hugging and crying. Mom broke us apart as soon as she saw a car coming down the road. It might hurt her reputation if people saw us crying in the driveway. I was beginning to think she really had no heart at all. She was so worried about what others would think, not her two daughters who had just had the life crushed out of them.

The next day my sister had to make all the arrangements for the funeral, so Mom and Dad were gone most of the day. My oldest brother came home that day, and that made the day a bit more bearable. He was seven years older than me, but he had been the one I felt closest to. When he moved away to go to university I lost my security blanket. He acted as a buffer between Mom and me when he could. When he moved away I was on my own, and I remember him apologizing to me one day because he wasn't there anymore. I was shocked. He had nothing to apologize for, certainly not for the actions of our mother. I wanted him to believe that, and I think eventually he did.

Because Jerry was so young, and had so many friends and relatives, there were two days of visitation at the funeral home before the funeral. I didn't want to go; I wasn't ready to accept it. I had no choice though, Mom made me go, all for the sake of the family appearance. So I spent two days staring at Jerry in his casket, knowing that when they closed it I would never see him again. I was so heartbroken. I wanted Bill with me, but he was working. Since we hadn't been dating very long it was bound to be awkward for him, meeting my extended family that way wasn't ideal, and I didn't want to put him through that. His family did send a beautiful bouquet of flowers, and when I called to thank his mom she said she hoped I got to bring the flowers home. I hoped that too. I did tell my dad that they wanted me to have it afterwards, and he said he would see what he could do.

The day of the funeral was so hard on me. I had lost my grandparents, and I had been as close to them as Jerry, but this was different. This was really the first time I understood what it meant, and I was very emotional. I had spent the night before with Bill and his family, and that had brought my spirits up some, and Bill called me the morning of the funeral to make sure I knew he was there in spirit with me. That was just one of the many reasons I loved him and his family.

It was time to get ready to go, and I was dragging my feet, trying to get my emotions under control. I tried, but it didn't work. I couldn't stop crying that day.

Before we all left the house Mom cornered me upstairs away from everyone. She had the nerve to say to me that I had better not cry that day because I would upset my sister. I'm sure my jaw hit the floor; I couldn't believe she would say that to me. But I had been warned. I knew there was no way I wasn't going to cry, I had been doing that for three days straight, and today was the worst day of all of them. Mom made me sit right beside her at the funeral, and every time she looked over and I was crying she pinched my leg. This was painful, and made me cry even harder. I knew I was in for it when she got me alone later. All of those emotions were just too much for me. I couldn't stop crying, even though I knew there were going to be big repercussions.

When we did get home I was able to keep away from Mom, and get out the door with Bill as soon as he got there. There were a lot of people at the house after the funeral, so Mom was distracted. But I knew it was going to be a big scene the next day when she caught up to me. Not only did I go against her by crying at the funeral, I had left with Bill shortly after. I didn't tell her, I told Dad, and Dad understood that I needed to get away. I assumed he would tell Mom later, which he did. Mom waited up for me. She was sitting alone in the living room reading her book, and as soon as I saw her face I knew I was in big, big trouble.

She used a yardstick on me. I had welts on my back, and I couldn't sit down comfortably. I had to hide the marks of course, because she would have a fit if I told anyone. When Bill and I went to his parent's weekend place Bill wanted to go swimming. I didn't know how I was going to hide the marks, so I put on a t-shirt over my bathing suit until we got to the pool. When we got in the pool I tried not to let Bill see my back. He came over to me in the water, and he knew that something was wrong with me. I hadn't been myself all day, but I couldn't tell him what had happened. I finally started to open up a little, and to tell him about Jerry's funeral and the way Mom acted towards me, and he put his arms around me to give me a hug.

All of a sudden he gasped, and pushed me away. It took me a few seconds to realize what was going on. He had felt the welts. He was mortified. I tried to shrug it off, and he did drop it for the time being. When we got back to the trailer he told his parents while I was changing. The looks on their faces told me that when I walked back in the room. They stopped talking, and just stared at me. Finally his mom got up and came over to me. She just hugged me tight, and told me she was so sorry. Before I knew it the four of us were hugging, and I was sobbing. They asked me if they could see my back, and I tried to talk my way out of it. I couldn't so I turned around and Bill pulled up my shirt for them to see. I thought that Bill had been mortified when he saw them, and he was, but his mom just burst into tears. His dad got angry, and said some things about my mother that I would never have expected to come out of his mouth. Then they asked me if I wanted them to call anyone. The police, Children's Aid, anyone that could help me out.

I was so scared I started to shake. They couldn't call anyone because it would just make it worse for me. I finally talked them out of it, and they said if they found out it happened again they were going to step in, no ifs ands or buts about it. It was nice knowing they were willing to stand up for me, and try to protect me, but at the same time I was terrified. I knew it would happen again, and I was scared what would happen if someone showed up at the door to talk to Mom. I knew that it would come back on me tenfold when she and I were alone again.

The rest of the summer I spent as much time with Bill as I could. We were inseparable. I know part of it was him protecting me in the only way he could by getting me out of the house and away from her. I thanked him for that over and over. His family truly was my salvation at that time. I had to live in the house with her for another two years before I graduated high school. Then I would be out of the house and gone to college. There was a light at the end of the tunnel, but it was a long way off.

That fall I started driver's education classes. There was one day when Mom actually asked me how it went, and I said not very well, my head just wasn't in it that day, and I seemed to make a lot of mistakes. She blew up. There was no excuse for that she said. When we got home I got the yardstick again. It wasn't as bad as the last time had been, but there were still welts on my back.

The next day at school after gym class the teacher called me to her office. She said she had seen my back, and wanted to know if I was okay. I begged her not to call anyone, especially Mom, and she agreed not to, but if she ever saw that kind of marks on me again she would have no choice but to call the authorities and have me removed from the house. I knew that would probably be better for me, but it was an unknown, and it scared me. I hoped that she wouldn't have to be put in the situation to call anyone.

Bill had the same reaction, and I begged him not to tell his parents. He said he wouldn't. That was a relief to me. I could always count on him to have my back, so to speak.

There was a day not long afterwards that my brother came home and walked into the kitchen. I could tell by the look on his face that he was mad, but I had no clue how mad, or who it was that he was mad at.

I found out in a hurry. He started to yell at me that I needed to shut my mouth, and stop telling people his girlfriend was pregnant. She had almost called off their engagement because of the rumour. I was dumbfounded, and pleaded with him to believe me. I would never start a rumour about anyone like that, and up until then I had thought that she and I were fairly close friends.

He stormed out again, before I could really defend myself, and I just stood there staring at the door.

Mom had been sitting at the kitchen table the whole time. She did not say one word, until I said that I didn't say it. All she said was that his girlfriend's sister should learn to keep her mouth shut.

What? She actually believed it wasn't me? I was astonished. But, why didn't she speak up when my brother was screaming at me? It was just another example of how little she really did care about me. I went to my bedroom and cried myself to sleep. That happened a lot.

Something changed in my Mom about that time. She stopped hitting me with the yardstick. The yelling and screaming was happening less as well. It was nice for a change. I never questioned it, but I always had the feeling that she got a call from someone. I never knew if it was my teacher, or Bill's parents. But someone had stepped in and threatened her, and she seemed to back down a little. Our relationship was so broken by that time that we only continued to grow farther and farther apart. By the time I was ready to leave for college she was like a stranger to me. I wasn't sad to leave her behind, but I did miss my Dad.

Chapter 62

I loved being out of the house and being at college. I had always put my all into school, it was the only thing I could do that seemed to pacify my Mom. At least I had good grades, and had graduated on the honour roll. Being out of the house forced me to look at myself, and really get to know the real me. I came into my own in college, and finally was able to figure out who I was and what I wanted out of life. Bill was still in my life, but towards the end of my first year he broke up with me. I was so heartbroken. He was my first love, and I missed him. We still talked once in a while, but it wasn't the same. I missed his family as well. They had taken me in and treated me like I was family to them, and I will never forget how safe they made me feel.

Bill asked me when I got home from college for the summer if I would like to meet his friend from work. It was a strange feeling to have my ex-boyfriend introduce me to someone new. It turned out to be a good thing though, and Tony and I ended up dating for almost four years. I was the one to end the relationship, and looking back I know now that I ended it because I was scared he would do it before me. I had issues with commitment, and an even bigger fear of someone leaving me. I know now it was more than likely because I felt rejected by both my birth mother and my adoptive mother. I wish I had figured it out then, and maybe my life would have turned out differently. When Tony and I split up I had no choice but to move back in with Mom and Dad. I had a full time job, and instantly started looking for an apartment, but for one long month I had to live there. It was great to be back with Dad, in fact we snuck away one day when I was home, and we went to the Porky Pig for ice cream. That had been our favourite spot when I was growing up. If I was able to go with Dad to the livestock auction we always stopped at the Porky Pig on the way home for ice cream. Going back there brought back many happy memories, and we were able to get there more than once in the next couple of years, until it closed.

Mom, however, was a different story. She couldn't lay a hand on me anymore, but she could belittle me. And that is what she spent the time doing, any chance she had. She couldn't believe I had two failed relationships before I was twenty-five. She was embarrassed when people asked her about me she said, and always tried to shrug it off and change the subject. She didn't want anyone to know that she had a daughter like me. We had a few screaming matches that month, but I came to realize it wasn't worth it. It wasn't worth the hurt I would feel, and I avoided her as much as possible. Thankfully I had my work, and my own car. I didn't have to spend time at home if I didn't want to, but, I didn't really have anywhere else to go. I would go to a park by the water, and try to sort my life out. That worked for a while.

During that time I met another man through my work. He was nice, and eventually asked me out. I accepted, and we went to a local bar for the evening. I wish I had seen the signs right away. But I didn't. He turned out to be an alcoholic, but we ended up married in spite of myself. I thought I could cure him. I couldn't. I didn't know any different at the time.

Mom didn't like my first husband, and told me so every chance she got. I was so tired of hearing everything negative that came out of her mouth that I almost told her not to come to my wedding. But she was there, and never smiled once. She was just so unbelievable. We were expected all our lives to put on the façade of being a happy family in public, yet she didn't have to live by the same rules. I was just glad that I wasn't living with her anymore, and we had very little contact.

My marriage lasted almost four years, and I really should have ended it sooner. I finally had to leave. I couldn't save him from himself, and he was just dragging me down with him. I had to save myself, and that's what I did. Of course it gave my Mom more fuel for her hatred of me. Now I was not only the one that couldn't keep a boyfriend, but I was going to be the first in her family to be divorced. We had such a huge fight shortly after I left him that I didn't call home for almost a year. As much as I missed my Dad that whole year, I couldn't deal with her. I was hurting, and trying to heal, and she was no good for me. It wasn't like I lost much of a relationship anyway.

Eventually I called home one day. I was missing my Dad a lot for some reason, and decided to call. Thankfully he answered the phone, and we had a good long chat. It was great to hear his voice, and to know that he had missed me as well. That connection between daddy and daughter was still there, no matter how much time passed. I was very grateful for that.

Life went on for the next few years on an even keel for me. I dated a few men, but nothing serious ever came of any of them. I wasn't ready for a serious relationship, so I shied away from anyone that got too pushy. I had had too much heartbreak, and I was trying to heal. I don't know that I ever healed, at least not before I met my second husband. That was Tom. Yes. That Tom. The one that is now married to my ex sister-in-law.

Chapter 63

So back to my life in Nanaimo. I spent months trying to work through all the feelings that had come up with the rejection from my birth mother. I needed that time to try to get past them, and one day it was like I had an epiphany. I could either let the two of them affect the rest of my life, or I could put them in my past and leave them there. I didn't need them to be fulfilled. It was their loss that they didn't want me in their lives. I had Charles and Ella. I had Emily and the family here. Almost overnight I became a different person. I was happy. I was almost bubbly. I found that I wasn't so tired all the time, and realized that I was ready to start dating again. I wasn't sure if I was ready for anything serious, but I had to dip my foot into the dating pool to find out.

I didn't know where a single woman my age went to meet men. There was a pub behind my apartment building that I had been to a few times, and I had met a few men there. I didn't know if they were dating material because until then I was not even entertaining the idea of dating.

I started to look at them differently now. I was friends with a lot of men, and I wondered if some of them were someone I would date. There was a couple that I thought I could date, but then I realized that if things went bad, I didn't want to lose their friendships. So I told them I was ready to start dating, and they, of course, had friends for me to meet.

I met some friends of my male friends, but no one really caught my attention. Dating was fun, but there was no one I could see in my future. Then my boss asked me out. We had gone out for drinks many times after work, just to wind down, and it was never anything more than friends and coworkers. In fact I had never looked at him as anyone I would ever date. That could be suicide in my job if we did date and it didn't work out, so before I said yes I told him we needed to talk about a few things. We both agreed that if it didn't work out, we could still remain friends because we had that foundation already.

It didn't work out.

I was miserable at work for a while. Not really because it didn't work out, but because he didn't hold up his end of the bargain. He treated me like I was his enemy, but we had talked when we both realized it wasn't going to work, and we promised each other there would be no blame from either person, and no animosity at work. I should have known. I was way too used to people breaking their promises to me.

I got over it quickly, and went out with a few more men. Again, nothing serious, I was just having fun, and I was clear about that to each and every one of them.

That was the summer of 2005. In August Becky had to come to Vancouver for a week for work. She wanted me to go over and spend some time with her. I jumped at the possibility, and arranged to have a couple of extra days off so I could go. I was there for four days, she was at work during the day, and I toured around, or just relaxed in the condo. We had a lot of fun that week, and it was just what I needed. I was refreshed when I got back home. I had a clear head, and was more open to dating, and possibly getting serious with someone. Becky had been like a therapist that week, and she helped me get through so many things I had been dwelling on, and letting them drag me down.

Chapter 64

Early in September I had gone over to the pub for a couple drinks one day after work. I was alone, and there was a man there that I had met a couple of times but never really talked to or knew anything about. He asked me if I wanted to sit with him since we were both alone, so I did. We had a lot of fun, talking, and getting to know one another. He walked me home when I left, and I found I couldn't get him out of my mind the next few days.

I decided I would go over one day again to the pub in the hopes that he was there. He was, and he said he was glad to see me again. I didn't let on that I had gone with the hope that he would be there. We had a great time again that day, and again he walked me home. This time I made sure I had his phone number, and he had mine. He asked me if I would like to go out for dinner one night, and I said of course.

We went to the pub a few days later, on our first official date. Since we were both regulars the staff thought it was so cute that we were on a date. They said we made a great couple. It was nice to be in a relationship again that seemed easy. We had fun together, and we seemed to want a lot of the same things. It didn't take long before we were in a serious relationship, and I had hopes of being happy once again.

Chapter 65

The new gentleman in my life is very good to me. His name is Damon. It wasn't many months into our relationship that we decided I should move in with him. It was a big step, but it felt right, so I gave my notice at my apartment, and started moving things to his house. I was incredibly happy. I had found the one good man left on the face of the earth. We were a great match.

Life with Damon was great. We didn't see a lot of each other because we were on opposite shifts. But on our days off we made up for lost time. We didn't have to go out all the time; we were comfortable at home alone, just spending time together. I felt like he could be the one that I spend the rest of my life with. I wasn't sure I wanted marriage, and neither was he, we were happy living together. It wasn't much different than marriage; we just hadn't made it "legal".

Damon is older than me, and has two grown children, and at that time had three grandchildren. One was just an infant, and his son's first child. His son and his girlfriend were getting married in the spring of 2006, and Damon asked me to go with him. His son and fiancé lived in Calgary then, so it was a great excuse to see my brother and his wife. We stayed with them for the week that we were in Calgary, and during the day we either visited with Damon's son and new baby, or just toured around the area, going to all of Damon's childhood haunts. It was a lot of fun learning about his past, and the wedding was fun.

When we got home from the wedding I ended up with a sinus and throat infection. My doctor said I was to be off work for a week. I let my manager know, and she was not very happy, but, there was nothing she could really do about it.

The next week my doctor said I was off for two more weeks. I just couldn't shake this infection, and my friends said I looked grey, and pale. No matter how much rest I got, I didn't seem to be getting any better. So back to the doctor I went, only to be told that I was going to be off work for at least another month. He tested me for everything he possibly could, but nothing showed up in the tests. That was when I heard the word fibromyalgia for the first time from my doctor. I went home in a daze, and read as much as I could on the internet about it. What I was reading worried me. It wasn't something that was going to go away if it turned out I had fibromyalgia. It was one of those conditions that doctors couldn't get a handle on because every patient had different symptoms.

Eventually he sent me to a rheumatologist in Victoria. She was a specialist in fibromyalgia and arthritis. There was a test that would tell her if I had it. She looked at my records that my doctor had sent her, and before she even examined me she said she was sure I had fibromyalgia, along with arthritis through much of my body.

The test to determine fibromyalgia was eighteen pressure points at nine bilateral locations on my body. She did the test, and told me that I had reactions at all of the pressure points, so it was definitely fibromyalgia. In the meantime I had been put on medical leave indefinitely, so I was on medical employment insurance for fourteen weeks, and when I wasn't able to go back at that time I had to apply for long term disability through work.

I was denied the benefits. I was furious. They had all the documentation saying that I could not do my job. I could not sit at a desk anymore, and with the medications I was now on, I could not stay awake for eight hours at a time. Being denied also meant that I had no income. I had to depend on Damon, and as much as he wouldn't say it, I didn't think it was fair to him to have to support me.

I didn't know what to do, and talked to Damon about it endlessly. It seemed like that was the end of the road for me, and I had no more options with the insurance company. One day I was feeling so desperate that I thought about calling the owner of the company I worked for. I wanted him to know that I had been denied benefits that I had been paying for, and they had been paying for as well. I didn't call him right away though; I wanted to talk to Damon first.

Damon thought I should do it. It couldn't hurt, and I wouldn't know what could happen if I didn't make the call. So the next day I called the owner of the company in Ontario. I had to leave a message as he wasn't in the office. I didn't say a lot in the message, just that I would like to talk to him about the benefits package.

The next day I heard from his private secretary, and she wanted all the details. She assured me that she would talk to him that day or the next, and would get back to me with whatever he had to say. I felt a little better that day, knowing I had at least done something about the situation. I didn't know what would come of it, but at least I had tried if nothing else.

Two days later I heard from the secretary again. She had talked with the owner about my situation and he asked her to pass along the message that he was going to do all he could to help me. He didn't know that there would be such a problem with the benefits package, and would definitely be meeting with the insurance representative to get to the bottom of the matter.

The beginning of the next week I heard from the insurance company. They had reviewed my file and were approving my benefits. I would be on long term disability for up to two years, and at that time if I was still unable to work they would help me with income options. I just laughed when I got off the phone. Apparently the owner, the top boss, had gone to bat for me. I was so excited that I would finally be able to contribute to the household again, and Damon was happy as well.

The next day I called to thank Mr. Stephens, the owner of the company, and left a voicemail for him. He personally returned my call later that day, and apologized for the trouble that the insurance company had caused me. I didn't think he needed to apologize, and I told him as much. Knowing what he had done for me made me feel lucky to work for a company like his. My boss in the office, however, was not impressed. He had received an email from the owner asking him why he wasn't looking after the employees in his office. I got an email telling me off basically, but I just ignored it. If he wanted to push the issue I might have to let slip that we had dated briefly, and let the chips fall where they may. He left it alone after a few more emails, and that was pretty much the last I ever heard from him.

I wanted to go back to work, but I didn't know what I could do. I couldn't take a job knowing that I would be setting myself up to fail basically. It wouldn't be fair to me, nor the employer. I searched the internet for jobs I could do from home, and one day I stumbled across a site for medical transcription. I researched it the next few days, making a few phone calls to schools that offered the course. The plus to the course was that I could do that from home as well.

Once I had all the information I needed I talked to Damon about it. He thought it was a great idea, and was totally supportive of me. I had never had that kind of unconditional support and love before, and when he acted in that manner I was still amazed. We had been together for over two years by that time, and we were still as happy as we ever had been. Every day I thanked my lucky stars for him. I didn't know why I had finally found him, but I wasn't going to let him go. He was exactly what I had been looking for all my life, and I finally felt content. I knew then that everything that had come before made me who I am, and brought him into my life when it was the right time.

Chapter 66

I applied for the medical transcriptionist course and for a student loan as well. I was approved for both, and started the course the next month. For a year I studied as much as I could. It was good for me to have a goal again. I had been in a state of depression previous to that because I was feeling rather worthless. This gave me purpose again.

A year later I had the certificate in my hand, and started looking for a job. I really thought it was something I could do because I had been able to do the course. What I didn't think of was that I had been able to do the course at my own speed. If I had a day where I couldn't do it, I took the day off. If I could only do a few hours one day, that was what I did. Looking for a job soon made me realize that I wasn't sure I could do it. I would have to work on their schedule, even though I would be working from home. I did try for a couple of months, and ended up making myself quite sick. I had a flare up of my fibromyalgia, and I realized then that I would probably never be able to work again. I sunk into depression again. It was a hard pill to swallow. Thankfully Damon was the man he was. He supported me, and didn't make me feel like I was a failure.

We had been living together for over three years at that time, and marriage had been mentioned a few times. I don't know that either of us was ready for it, but we tossed the idea around once in a while.

In January of 2009 we took the plunge. We went to a Marriage Commissioner and were married. We were incredibly happy, and started to think about selling the house, and getting a place that was both of ours.

We decided a month later to list our house, and started looking at places we might want to move to. We had decided on a retirement type area, instead of across from an elementary school like we were at that time. We had an offer right away on the house, so we decided it was best to start packing. The move might come sooner than we thought.

The first offer fell through which was a bit of a letdown, but our realtor assured us it would still sell quickly. He was right. It sold within four months, and at a time when the real estate market had dropped off. So we found a modular home park that was about the newest park in the city. It was immaculately kept, and we fell in love with it. We found a couple places that were for sale that we wanted to see right away. When we left the first one we didn't need to see anymore. As far as we were concerned we had found our new home. We put in an offer that evening. The owners counter offered within hours, and we slept on it overnight. The next day we put in another counter offer, and finally came to an agreement with the owners. We were really moving. I was excited. It would be less work than the house and a lot less yard work as well. It was perfect. We had a month to pack and be ready to move. It was a busy month between packing, and keeping up with life. By the time the day of the move arrived I was exhausted, and knew that I had to turn around and unpack it all. I hoped that being in the new place would motivate me to unpack and try to ignore the fact that I was exhausted.

I had the new place unpacked and settled within the first week. Damon helped when he could, but was working as well, so I did the majority of it, which was fine with me. I took my time, and was satisfied with the end results. There weren't many changes we made to where I had originally put things. Finally we were able to relax, and start our new life. It was a great time for us.

Once we were settled, and I took some time to rest and recover, I had to start thinking again about working. I went to the doctor to talk to him about it, and he told me that maybe I needed to consider "early retirement". He was referring to the government disability pension. He didn't like to call it a disability because of the negative connotation and that was why he called it retirement. I liked the sound of that better than being disabled.

So I started the paperwork to apply for the disability pension. I had to gather doctor's reports, and work reports. I had to get people that knew me well to write letters describing my abilities. It was a lot of paperwork, but I got it all together and mailed it off. It could take up to six months to hear whether I was accepted or declined. I had been told that most people got turned down the first time just on principle. It was viewed by many people as the government's way of weeding out the people that weren't seriously in need of benefits. When I got the letter that my application was declined I was upset, but not all that surprised. So it was on to round two.

Chapter 67

I had to gather more paperwork to support my need for the disability pension. That took some time, but I got it all together and sent it off again. It was time to wait for the government wheels to turn now. All I could do was wait again.

I felt like it had more significance this time. If I was declined I would have to go in front of a panel of three people to argue my case for needing the pension. There would be a ministry representative there as well to add any more reasons that they may have for declining me again.

It felt like a long wait, and I waited three months to find out that I was declined again. Round three was coming up. It was time for the hearing. I sent in the paperwork saying I wanted the hearing, and waited for a letter back to let me know what the process was now.

When the letter came that described the process and what I needed to do to be ready for it, it seemed like I had a good chance of being approved finally. It took another four or five months to get the date, which was another few months away. I found out closer to the date who would be on the panel that would decide my fate. There was going to be a lawyer, a business man, and a nurse. I was nervous, but kept telling myself that I would win this round.

The day of the hearing Damon went with me. The questions I expected to hear were not the ones they had at all. They wanted to know what a day in my life looked like, and why I couldn't hold down a job. The nurse wanted to know all the medications I was on, and how they affected me. Did I need to have a nap every day because of the strength of the meds, and questions like that were what they asked. I felt like it went well. If they listened to me, they would hear that I couldn't make it through a whole day without some kind of rest, and that the strength of the medications I was on would definitely hinder my abilities to concentrate on any kind of job. Damon had a chance to give his opinions on why I should be approved, and we both left feeling optimistic. We had to keep that optimism going over the next few months. It wasn't all that easy, and I had some dark days. If I was declined again, I had no more options as far as I could tell, and Damon kept telling me not to worry about it until I had to. I tried but it wasn't easy.

After a few months of waiting, on a Friday afternoon I got a notice in the mail that I could pick up my registered letter from the government on Monday. It was the decision, and it had taken another six months to get this far. I didn't want to wait until Monday if I didn't have to, so I called the outlet where the letter would be delivered to later that day. The young man working there told me to call back after 5 p.m. and if it was there I could pick it up then and not have to wait until Monday.

Five o'clock couldn't come fast enough that day. I called right away, and he told me that it was there. We went to the drugstore to get the package, and I tore into it as soon as I was back in the car. They had approved me for the pension. I was finally going to have an income again, which would take some of the pressure off Damon having to cover everything. The bonus of being approved was that it was retroactive to when I had applied. So my first cheque was rather substantial. We put most of the money into the house. New floors all throughout, new appliances, new bed, and some new furniture. The best purchase we made was a puppy.

It was a great weekend. We were certainly happy knowing that it was over, and time to move on to the next chapter of our life.

Chapter 68

It is 2013 now, and we have celebrated our fourth wedding anniversary. I am a fulltime homemaker, and Damon has retired. Our life is peaceful and comfortable. We live a quiet life, which is fine with me. I still have flare ups of my fibromyalgia, but not as often, and sometimes not as severe as the last one. I know my limitations and I try not to push the boundaries if I can help it.

There have been many ups and downs in my life, maybe no more than anyone else has had in their lives, but these are mine. All of these parts of my life have made me the person that I am today. I could have chosen to be bitter, and, really, who could blame me? I have not had an easy life. But instead of dwelling on all the negativity, I choose to cut those parts of my life out. Again, it's their loss.

I surround myself with positive energy these days. So if you're coming to my door with negative energy you have two choices. Either you can leave it at the door, or you can turn around and walk away because you won't be welcome.

Sometimes it takes a lot of work to stay positive, but I do the work. When I feel down, when I feel like I have been dealt a bad hand, I look around me at what I do have. A beautiful island, a beautiful home, and a beautiful life with Damon and our two fur babies. There's nothing like the love of a good man and the two bundles of joy that Scrappy and Marley are. I also have two step children and four grandchildren. Life is good.

It has taken me forty-seven years to get to this point, and it's been a long road. It seems like most of it was an uphill battle, and I can say that I may not have won all the battles, but I do feel like I have won the war. Marley turned two years old in March, and she is a Morkie, a mix of Yorkshire Terrier and Maltese. She is an active puppy, but I love having her around. Scrappy is seven, and he is a Silky Terrier. He wasn't too accepting of Marley when we brought her home. She was only eight weeks old at the time, and the more active she became the more Scrappy thought she should go back to where she came from. She has been with us for over two years now, and they get along much better now. Our little family is a tight unit, and we wouldn't have it any other way.

I don't think about my mothers very often. They made their decisions, and I have accepted them the best I can. To be honest, I feel that it is their loss that they don't want me in their lives. They are missing out on a great person, their daughter. It's too bad for them. I love my life, and they can't knock me down again. Writing this has been like therapy for me. There have been highs and lows in the process, but they were all necessary and I have dealt with them as they came up. Now my mothers are completely in my past, and until they come to me with better attitudes toward me they will no longer occupy any time in my life.

Damon is a Buddhist, and over the years I have taken an interest in learning about it. I do volunteer transcription for a magazine that focuses on Buddhism and other religions like it, and I find the lessons that I have learned from the transcriptions, along with the things that Damon has taught me, have completed the circle and finally brought me into my own. Without those lessons I don't know where I would be, but it wouldn't be in such a happy place I'm sure.

I have gone from a broken, lost, frightened little girl, to a positive, confident woman who has found her voice and who she is. I am proud of how far I have come.

From lost to found.

It is now time for me to rejoin my family and our wonderful life. I think we will go walk the dogs in the forest. They have missed me I'm sure. So has my husband. I am going to make that all up to them somehow, and soon. In fact, that starts right now.

THE END

Brenda Seymour is a 47 year old homemaker residing in Nanaimo, British Columbia. She was raised in Monkton, Ontario, a small farming community, and moved to Nanaimo in 2003. Her mother was a librarian and books have always been a huge part of her life. Writing seemed like the natural progression, which she now enjoys as a hobby. In her spare time Brenda can be found on the trails of Nanaimo with her husband and two small dogs, Scruffy & Trixie; or at home spending time with her hedgehog, Tumbleweed.